The Original's Rage

David Watkins

Original Books

Published by Original Books

ISBN: 978-1068782206 (print)

ISBN: 978-1068782213 (ebook)

For Tinu (again)
The One.
Always.
Also, for Ed.
Rest easy, big guy.

Prologue

Sunday afternoon – Losthorn, Scotland

The boat drifted, anchor holding it so it wouldn't move too far. A lone figure cast a line deep into the water, and sat back, letting the rare early spring sun warm his face. His dark hair was dusted with grey – salt and pepper, his wife called it, and his face showed a few thin lines which would deepen into grooves before too long. He was a handsome man with a solid build and not an ounce of fat on him; his wife said he was ageing like a fine wine. She was biased, of course. The move to Scotland had been good for him though, that was for sure.

For a start, he hadn't killed anyone for nearly ten years.

Salmon didn't count, however. His line twitched but went still again. He smiled to himself. Soon. He could've used *other* methods, but that just didn't seem fair to the fish.

His family was much happier now too – settled in, making friends in the village. He was slower to make friends, but then, he wasn't as friendly as he'd once been. Being on the run did that to you. Shadows everywhere. You never knew who had an ulterior motive. Bit like Clarkey.

The man had a twinge of regret at thinking about Clarkey, but he'd had to go. He'd been too much of a risk – unknown, volatile, probably dangerous. Pretty simple really.

Now the line whizzed off the spool, rod bending towards the water, and he gripped it firmly with both hands. He was strong enough to have handled the fish with one, but it might have looked a mite suspicious to any onlookers. Still, it didn't take long to reel in, and the gleaming salmon thudded onto the boards.

It looked a good size too, maybe ninety centimetres long, maybe a shade less. Around ten kilos. The man smiled. They would eat well tonight. He smacked its head on the wooden seat, killing it, then sliced his knife through the gills - just to be sure - before placing the salmon in a bucket.

He took a moment to admire the shoreline with rolling green hills in the distance and larger mountains beyond. Behind him, the loch opened via a narrow channel in a natural sea wall to the wild North Sea. His tiny rowing boat would not have lasted long out there, not even on a relatively calm day like today. He pulled up the anchor and started rowing for shore.

Powerful strokes made the boat sing through the water, and he grinned. Hot sun in Scotland, a clear blue sky above, fresh salmon for dinner, a beautiful woman and handsome boy at home.

Jack Stadler's smile grew.

Life was good.

CHAPTER 1

Sunday evening – South-East London

1

Flo sank into the sofa, letting its soft cushions hug her. A smile greased her lips, and she closed her eyes. Her muscles relaxed and the immediate pressure faded. The squalor of the flat became an irrelevance as bliss overtook her.

She could feel Harry's eyes on her and pictured his handsome, caring face, with his brow furrowed and lips tense. He didn't need any drugs to control himself, but then he was better at it than her. She'd brought him to this life, and he'd taken to it like a rabid dog.

A giggle escaped her lips. She opened her eyes, her gaze meeting Harry's intense stare. He didn't smile, but she felt her heart sing at the sight of him. She wanted his big strong arms around her, wanted his lips against hers, but they were surrounded by the others so she'd have to wait.

Someday, he will be the father of my children. Beautiful they'll be - two boys and a girl.

She dropped the needle, letting it slip out of her hand as the high took hold and she closed her eyes again.

2

Harry watched the smile grow on her face. Helplessness overtook him, replacing the anxiety he'd felt as the needle slide into her arm. This was a new thing for them both, something Harry had yet to partake in. For now, and for him, spliffs were enough to keep the wolf from the door.

He had to look somewhere other than his high-as-a-kite wife. The flat was small, far too small for the seven people currently in there. Two sofas dominated the living room, leaving no room for any other furniture except the expensive television hanging from a bracket on the wall. It loomed over them, drawing everyone's gaze as surely as the tractor-beam of the Death Star even though it was muted. A soap was on it at the moment, some pretty young actress mouthing silent words in 4K high def.

Gary can afford a TV like that but not a cleaner? Jesus.

Harry was squashed on the sofa between two bigger men – the brothers Chris and Rich. The Chuckle Brothers, Flo called them, mostly because, well, they just didn't. They'd joined the group a couple of weeks ago. Chris was slightly bigger, slightly more amiable – although that was like saying a tiger was friendlier than a shark. Rich's eyes were dark pits, devoid of emotion. Flo looked past that, however, saying everyone should be allowed to join the group, so here they were.

Opposite, Flo sat between Freddie and Alex. Harry wasn't sure of their relationship, but Alex definitely did enough to keep Freddie keen. All she had to do was give him a look, all eyelashes and doe eyes, and he did whatever she asked. He was like a puppy in her presence.

Kind of fitting, really.

Gary sat on a chair he'd dragged in from the kitchen, somehow squeezing it into a gap between the sofas, grinning at all his visitors like he'd never had company. *Hell, the state of this place, he probably hasn't.* He held a spliff, dragging on it with a loud, wet, sucking noise.

Harry didn't fancy the next toke on that.

Behind Gary, a galley kitchen full of dirty plates and cups threatened to tumble to the floor. Beyond that, a short corridor led to the bedroom and bathroom and back to the front door. *Well, there's no back door, so maybe just* door *would be more accurate.* The whole flat had a depressing air: poor and desperate, matching the people in it.

Harry could hear the television and stereo competing next door, presumably from different rooms. He didn't need sensitive hearing for that – the walls were so thin, he could probably punch through it. The flat was on the third floor of twenty. Outside the front door – which was surprisingly robust – a long balcony ran the length of the building. Two flights of stairs gave access at both ends, with a lift in the middle. He liked the two flights of stairs – limited exits always made him nervous, and it was good to have options.

He and Flo had come up in the lift. The smell of urine threatened to overwhelm them both. He really didn't need enhanced senses to appreciate how grim the odour was. Not an experience he would ever repeat. He shuddered. Of course, the stairwells smelt just as bad, but at least out there you had a chance of fresh air. No-one knew Gary until he'd put a message out saying he'd found a safe house. Chris and Rich talked about it first, persuading the others to move on from the house in Sidcup.

They'd all been looking for a new place anyway. Flo didn't like to stay anywhere too long, and they'd been in Sidcup for three months. It had started to feel like a home, but Rich came home one night saying he'd been followed and that was that.

The group had separated to travel – less conspicuous in pairs – and Flo and Harry were the last to arrive at this shithole. The drugs started in Sidcup and Harry felt sick to see her continue with them now.

Rich offered him the spliff, passing it straight on from Gary. *He doesn't want that wet end either.* Harry took it, enjoying the fumes for a moment, but passed it straight on to Chris without putting it to his lips. Chris took a drag, pulled a face, but kept the spliff anyway.

"You sure this place is safe?" Freddie said. It was the third time he'd asked that in the last twenty minutes.

Gary nodded, his pupils huge – a combination of the drugs and the dim light. "Yeah, totally, mate. No-one has a clue we're here. We can have a little R&R yeah?"

"Whatever, man."

"This stuff'll kill you." Chris said, passing the spliff back to Gary. "Make you slow."

"Nah man, won't kill me." He grinned. "I've been there once."

Harry frowned. *What the hell was he talking about?* His expression must have matched his thoughts, as Gary kept talking.

"I used to live in Scotland, see, wee laddie." He said the last in one of the worst attempts at a Scottish accent Harry had ever heard. "Lived in a commune, for a bit, before all this. It was alright, not enough sex, like, it wasn't like the films." Harry had no clue what films Gary was talking about. *Pornos probably.* Gary waved the spliff around, using it to punctuate his points. "Made some friends, took care of the property, that kind of thing." Big drag and long exhale. "Anyway, smoked like a chimney I did, ciggies, one of them shit vape things, anything I could inhale really."

"Why are you telling us this?" Harry was losing patience. He wanted to bundle Flo up and go find somewhere else to stay for the night.

"I'll get there mate, let me tell it in my way." Gary grinned and Harry fought the urge to knock his teeth out. "Anyways, got the big C didn't I? The old cancer and I thought I was done for. Riddled in me lungs, and it had spread to my lymphatic system." It took him three attempts to pronounce 'lymphatic' correctly.

"Get to the point mate, for fuck's sake," Rich said.

Gary's grin widened. "I got healed, didn't I? By one of us."

3

Captain Peter Knowles sat in the van, headphones in, listening to the inane chatter. He removed them when he heard *'Get to the point for fuck's sake'* and looked at his team. He tried to smile, but even that simple act was proving harder and harder these days.

"Okay, we're a go. Suspects confirmed at location. This is real."

His squad all nodded.

Jesus, they all look about twelve. Every single one of them was new to his unit. They'd all volunteered too, which, given the shit storm of Exeter, meant they were all fairly stupid. Did any of them really understand what they were letting themselves in for? *Alpha team. How ironic. Shit, nothing alpha about them.*

He grabbed a tablet and used it to broadcast to the internal TV in their van. There was an identical device in a matching van, where Bravo team were watching and listening. A schematic of the flats appeared. Knowles fumbled with his laser pointer, until the red dot appeared on the screen. Sometimes, he hated being in charge, using all this modern technology. He felt the eyes of his team bore into him.

"Two stairwells so these are the only routes out, bar the lifts. Bravo team, I want eyes here and here." He indicated the two entrances at the bottom of the stairwells, then pointed at a square halfway between them. "Lift here - I want it shut down. Nothing fancy. Get the lift to the ground floor and wedge the doors open. As soon as this starts, if *anyone* comes out, they get detained." He paused, waiting for a protest. It didn't come. *Good.* "These two flats are to be emptied." The flats either side of the one the wolves were in. "We get people out quickly and quietly."

A hand went up. Towner. *Always fucking Towner.*

"Rest of the flats?"

Knowles shook his head. "The longer we're up there, the greater the chance of detection."

"What if they resist?" Miller said. One of the youngest. *Maybe his balls would drop by the end of this op.*

"They won't." This from Towner. He looked like he needed garden shears to shave. Towner pointed at his weapon to show what he meant. Miller frowned, swallowed once and nodded. He gripped his own weapon a little tighter.

"Anyone resists we put them down," Knowles said. "We're not here to play it safe. That said, people are jumpy right now, and you still need to be courteous. You are removing them from their homes on a Sunday night. Most of them will be getting ready for school or work."

"Round here?" Penfold snorted. The only woman on his team. Bravo had three. Something else for him to sort when he got back to base. He needed more women, not only to balance the testosterone, but they made for better soldiers in this sort of situation. Penfold, was hard as nails, and respected by the others. *Most of them.*

Her comment drew sniggers from Towner and Rawson. Knowles glared at them and cut the feed to the other van. "Game faces folks. This is serious. Have any of you seen a wolf up close?"

They all averted their eyes, except Towner.

"I have." Knowles removed his cap and ran a hand through his hair. "I've seen them tear people apart. I've seen them rip through an entire base full of people. I've seen them attack a village where anyone who survived was lucky. Do not underestimate them."

"Weren't you in Exeter as well, sir?" Towner said. He was still eyeballing Knowles.

Knowles nodded.

"You're pretty unlucky then sir, aren't you?"

This drew sniggers, but the rest of the squad knew enough to stay silent.

"Why did you volunteer to be part of my unit?" Knowles said. His voice was quiet, calm, masking the fury underneath.

"I wanted to bag a wolf, sir. Get its head for the wall in my dad's shed." Towner's smirk was built for punching the shit out of.

"You're going to get your chance tonight, but I really hope you don't see one up close." Knowles leant forward. "They're *not* pretty. They're *not* cool. They *are* killing machines that will think nothing of putting you – all of you – down, unless you beat them to it."

He looked at each person in turn, then returned to staring at Towner. "I watched one of those things gut my friends. It didn't stop, even with a bullet in it. There are seven of them up there. Just one is enough to kill us all – both squads. You need to focus on that and cut the macho bullshit, or you will die tonight. Screaming. Holding your guts in and praying for it to take your throat next just so the pain will end and you don't end up like one of them."

He stared at Towner, making the other man uncomfortable. Waiting for the silence to stretch to an unbearable level. Jack had told him about using that technique with naughty kids in school. Knowles snorted. Jack fucking Stadler. He hadn't even thought of Jack in years so why the hell was he using his advice?

"Yes sir," Towner said eventually. "On it, sir." To his credit, it looked like he meant it.

"Good." Knowles ran a hand through his hair again. It hadn't got any thicker. "Look, Towner, all of you, just be careful. Intel came from a message intercepted by the team in Kent. There's only meant to be three wolves, plus the flat owner up there. We don't know if he's a wolf or not. Someone, somewhere, has forgotten how to count and we have seven targets. Do not take any chances. If in doubt, put them down. I want us all back on base drinking hot fucking chocolate by lunch, okay?"

Never make promises. Jesus, Knowles, you're losing your touch.

4

"So, I went back to the commune, basically to die, like. But there was a bloke there. A wolf, but not normal. Special he was. He healed me he did. Just like a fuggin' shaman or something, you know, like an Indian?"

Harry glanced at Rich. *What the hell was this twat going on about?*

Rich, however, didn't return the look. He'd locked eyes with his brother, a strange expression on his face. It took Harry a minute to realise Rich was *smiling.* Chris too.

"Yeah, he bit me, he did. I was already a wolf see, but he bit me anyway. Turns out his bite has this thing, this stuff in it."

Gary took another huge, wet drag, put his head back and blew out smoke. When he was done, he grinned at the others.

"Hurt like hell it did, but it worked. No more cancer for me."

5

Knowles put the headphones back in, and heard an unknown male say, '....cancer for me.'

He frowned and kept listening.

6

Miller was on point. He should have felt honoured, but really, his stomach was a hot, boiling mess and he was pretty sure everybody could see how much he was shaking. The barrel of his SA80 seemed to wave around more than when his dad used to play those old FPS games on the PlayStation.

He crept past Bravo team. Two stood each side of the stairwell, weapons primed and ready. One nodded as he passed, but the others remained vigilant. If he did his job properly, they wouldn't be needed. Still, good to know they were there.

Miller crept into the stairwell, recoiling as the acrid stench of urine hit him. Towner followed and gagged.

"Fuck's sake," he said.

"Quiet."

Miller had been about to speak but Knowles beat him to it. Instead, he glared at Towner and all he got was a smirk and an eye roll. Towner pointed at the mics they all wore and made the dickhead gesture.

Miller turned away. Knowles seemed alright to him, and Towner one of those blokes who hated authority no matter what. Miller had seen loads of people like that in school, and every single one of *them* had actually been a dickhead.

His boots felt heavy on his feet as they climbed the stairs. All that training, all that effort and he felt like he wouldn't even make it three flights up. Wasn't adrenaline supposed to have kicked in by now?

Graffiti covered every part of the stairwell – even the stairs themselves. Most of it consisted of indecipherable tags, names in hearts or calling someone a slag. Another bit of graffiti said *'All tories are cunts'*. Towner kissed two fingers and pressed them to the sign. Some kindred spirits here.

Third floor. Fresh air blew away the worst of the stench. Miller pulled out a fibre optic cable and pushed it round the corner, onto the long narrow balcony. He gazed at a screen for a second or two, seeing the faceless, identical doorways stretch the length of the balcony, then he gave Towner a thumbs up.

All clear.

They slid onto the balcony, Towner leading the way to the first door. Miller crept along behind him, weapon now in place, locked into his shoulder. Towner stayed to Miller's right, moving so they both had a clear view ahead.

At the other end of the balcony, Penfold and Rawson headed towards them, in the same cautious advance.

They reached the flats either side of the target at the same time. Towner rapped on the door softly. No way that would be heard over the TV surely? Miller glanced over at Penfold who was already directing a family to the stairwell. A tired looking couple with a toddler, all pale at the sight of the armed – and clearly not police – force on their doorstep, ran for the stairwell, Rawson following them. He stopped at the top of the stairs, watching the family descend.

"Come on, come on," Towner muttered, and knocked again.

7

Harry's head snapped up. *What the hell was that noise?*

Rich heard it too. No-one else moved, just continued chatting and smoking the spliffs. Flo was out for the count, eyes half closed, blissful smile still in place.

Harry stood and crossed to the kitchen, staring down the corridor. Bedroom and bathroom doors were closed on the right-hand side. The other door to the sitting room sat open on the left. The front door, covered in yellowing white gloss, peeling and flaking with age, stood closed.

"Hey man," Gary said, "where're you going? Have some smoke, man."

He started giggling, but Harry ignored him.

"Need to finish me story, don't I?"

Harry stared at the front door, listening. Nothing moved in the flat bar the hazy wisps of smoke. Next door had moved on to a quiz show.

What's the capital of Australia?

But nothing from the left-hand neighbour. No more shouting at each other. Maybe they were in a bout of make-up sex? He shook his head – that he'd be able to hear.

Sydney. Two voices, a man's from the flat itself and a woman's from the TV.

Freddie arrived at his side. He took his t-shirt off and started unbuttoning his jeans. Harry frowned at him, but Freddie shrugged. "I like this shirt. Better safe."

Oh no, I'm sorry, it's Canberra.

"Ha, ha, dickhead. You're thick as shit."

"Fuck off, at least I had a go."

Freddie took a step towards the door.

8

"I like this shirt. Better safe."

Knowles leaned back in his chair. *What the hell does that mean?* It hit him like a brick.

"You've been made. Go now. Go! Go! Go!"

9

Knowles was shouting in his ear, but Miller couldn't focus on anything, His vision was blurred, his chest felt tight, and his legs trembled. Towner stopped rapping on the door and turned towards the target flat.

Behind him, the door opened, revealing a burly man with a scowl so ingrained on his face it looked tattooed.

"What the fuck?" the man bellowed.

Towner put a finger to his lips, and the man stared at him like he was speaking Dutch.

"Who is it?" A woman's voice, from deep in the flat, just about audible over the blare of the television.

"Out, now." Towner's voice made it plain he would not be argued with, although the SA80 probably made a more persuasive point. "Quickly, we don't have time to fuck about."

Miller took his eyes off the door, and that's all it took.

10

Freddie changed and jumped at the door, shattering it. Splinters flew out onto the balcony, as the broken door leapt from its frame. It smacked into the wall opposite, and spun over it, dropping the three storeys to the concrete car park below. He skidded onto the balcony and howled.

A young man crouched in front of him, wearing a black uniform. He clutched a mean looking gun to his shoulder, but the barrel was shaking. He should have fired by now but didn't. Freddie swiped with a huge paw, raking claws across the man's face and sending him crashing into the wall. The gun clattered loose from the soldier's grip, skidding across the balcony, stopping at his feet.

Freddie changed back to his human form, feeling the cool air bite at his naked skin. He picked the gun up.

11

Harry ran to Flo and shook her. Her eyes drifted open and her grin broadened when she saw him.

"Love you," she said, words muffled like she'd stuffed a load of cotton wool in her mouth.

"Yeah, I know." He tried to pull her off the sofa, but she resisted, flopping back onto the cushions. "We gotta go, babe."

Outside, gunfire.

12

Knowles hit his mic. "Bravo, stay put. Do not move from your positions. Nobody gets out of those flat unless they're wearing black – do you copy?"

Shaky voices replied in the affirmative.

"Towner. Miller. Give me a sit-rep."

Nothing.

Gunfire rattled over the mic, and Knowles pulled his headset off. He grabbed the nearest SA80 and was out of the van and running before the shooting stopped.

13

Penfold ran the length of the corridor, boots thudding with each step. Rawson followed, shouting at people to return to their flats. Ahead, Miller hit the wall, and even this far away, Penfold could see blood spatter onto the concrete.

14

Towner opened fire as the naked man picked up the weapon. He kept the trigger depressed for longer than he had to as round after round smacked into the guy. The man collapsed, bleeding from wounds no surgeon could repair. Towner stepped towards him, remembering his training.

One in the head.

Always one in the head.

15

Gary stood up, his eyes wide with surprise. "What the f—"

"We've been made!" Alex screeched, drowning out Gary. "Oh god! Freddie help me!"

Had she seriously not realised he'd already gone?

"Move!" Harry yelled and he dragged Flo more forcibly from the couch. She staggered and he held her up. "Can you change?"

She grinned at him, but her eyes told the truth.

16

Miller grunted and held a hand to his face. Blood coursed through his fingers, and pain flared around the wound. Somewhere in the fight – and how laughable a description *that* was – he had pissed himself. At least with everything else going on, no-one would notice. Jesus his face hurt.

"You're alive," Towner said. He'd just put a round in the naked guy's head. "Stay down, man, give us cover." He slid Miller's weapon back to him. "Don't worry, I won't tell anyone you pissed yourself."

Miller found he didn't care. His face hurt too much. He lifted the SA80 with one hand but kept the other pressed to his face. Penfold arrived and knelt beside him, fumbling with a pack at her waist. Soon a gauze pad was pressed to his face and Penfold roughly strapped it to his head.

"Okay?"

Miller nodded, but the barrel of his weapon still shook.

Behind Rawson, Towner entered the flat.

17

"Come on babe, please!" Harry dragged Flo now, but the high was showing no sign of wearing off. It must have been stronger than she was used to. He heard something roll into the living room, and saw the grenade stop by the sofa he'd just left.

He turned Flo away as it went off.

18

"Flashbang," Towner mouthed and rolled the grenade into the living room. Both he and Penfold turned away, shielded by the walls either side of the doorway. Their earpieces protected them from the worst of the bang, and goggles against the flash.

19

He couldn't see anything. Everything was white and indistinct, but Harry knew he was lying on top of Flo. The blast had knocked them over, and by the screaming, it had done far worse to Gary. Harry registered it had been a flashbang, rather than a grenade, but the heat and force of the blast had still been enough to take Gary down.

He didn't know where the others were. Last he'd seen, Alex was still sat on the sofa, but surely she'd moved by now? Surely?

Footsteps in the corridor.

The soldiers were coming in. Even as the thought formed, he knew he was wrong.

The soldiers were already here.

20

Towner scanned the room, taking in all the details whilst the occupants were still disorientated by the flashbang. A man lay on his side near a door through to what looked like the most disgusting kitchen he's ever seen. His leg was shredded below the knee, and he howled in agony.

Next to him on a dirty sofa, a pretty woman tried to get to her feet. She was blinking rapidly, but that wasn't going to do anything about the flashbang aftereffects. Her movements were sluggish, and she staggered.

Towner didn't hesitate. He opened fire, hitting her in the head. Another shot also put the man down.

This bagging wolves thing is a piece of piss.

21

Harry heard the bark of the gun and braced himself.

Nothing.

No searing pain. No shouts either.

The effects of the flashbang were fading, and he realised he was in the kitchen. He must have pushed Flo into the worst room in the flat, before the flashbang went off. They didn't have long before the soldier spotted them.

Where the hell was Rich? Chris?

He looked up, seeing the corridor. The soldier had moved into the sitting room, but Harry could see the edge of his bulky frame in the doorway. Opposite, the door to the bedroom was open. *Weird, it was shut earlier.* Dust filled the air coming from the bedroom. The shadow in the doorway moved, disappearing further into the living room.

"Let's go," he said, dragging Flo to her feet and running for the bedroom.

22

Movement, to his left.

Towner turned and fired, but the wolves were too quick. Plates shattered under the onslaught of his rounds, sending lumps of days old food flying through the air. He ran into the kitchen, heading after the wolves.

23

Rawson ushered the man and his screeching wife out of the flat next door. They should have already been moved, but everything had gone South so quickly. Next to him, Penfold tended to Miller's wounds and Towner had gone all *John Wick* on them, heading into the flat by himself. At least the family were heading for safety, their grown-up sons running out last, heading down the long balcony. The parents wore expressions of shock and terror, but the sons looked like they were enjoying themselves. *How the hell did that flat hold all those people?*

"Four civvies coming down," he said into his mic.

"Copy that."

Rawson knelt against the doorframe, liking the feel of the cold, solid wall next to him.

24

An optimistic double bed dominated the small room and above the headboard, a large hole wrecked the back wall. *Thank you, shitty workmen and shitty landlords.* Harry dragged Flo through the crude hole, breaking more of the plasterwork as he went.

The flat they entered was the mirror layout of Gary's one, so they were in the bedroom. Flo was blinking rapidly, her pupils returning to normal size. The drugs were wearing off already. She was already needing her fixes much more quickly. *Christ.*

"Alex?"

"Dead, I think. We don't have time right now. Keep moving."

He pulled her into this flat's kitchen – a much cleaner room, but it still stank of grease and deep-fried food. Nothing moved in the flat, save the dust swirling around their heads. He couldn't hear anything, so the TV and stereo had been switched off at some point. *Where were the people?* He could see through the flat, out onto the balcony.

A soldier knelt by the door; his attention taken by the other flat.

"I need you to run," Harry said. "I'll meet you downstairs."

"No," she said. "Don't leave me."

"I'm not." He touched her face, then smiled. "Just run when the screaming starts."

25

Towner crept through the hole, moving with caution. He swept the bedroom, aiming down his sights the whole time. *Clear.* He checked the doorway and saw the wolves. Towner had them both in his sights. They had no clue he was there. He grinned to himself. *Awesome.*

Then the man changed into a wolf, and Towner started shaking. He couldn't help it. *It's not real. Can't be real.* Warm liquid streamed down his leg and his mouth was dry.

The wolf was huge. It filled the corridor, muscles rippling along its back, visible despite the thick black fur coating it. It had seemed to burst out of the man – exploding out of his skin.

Easily the most terrifying thing Towner had ever seen.

The wolf bounded towards the open door and the woman sprinted after it.

26

Rawson heard heavy footsteps and a low growl and turned towards the flat. A huge black wolf hit him in the groin. It lifted its head, carrying him towards the wall, like a bull with a matador. Rawson screamed and hit the wolf's head. He may as well have been punching jelly, for all the good it did. His weapon fell from his hand, bouncing on the concrete.

They hit the balcony wall, the one that was surely too low to pass any health and safety inspection, and spun, crashing over it.

Rawson fell.

Wind rushed past his head, giving him just enough time to realise what was about to happen. Rawson landed headfirst on a car roof with enough force to shatter its windows and dent its roof.

The last thing that went through his mind was his spine.

27

Knowles shouted at Bravo team, screaming to not let anyone out, even as they shepherded a family out of the stairwell. The family ran to the far end of the car park, mother and father clutching each other as they went. The two sons followed closely, both grinning like fools. Curtains twitched behind them – neighbours gawping at the action.

"Get over to them!"

His yells fell on deaf ears, and then one of his men landed headfirst on a car roof. Knowles skidded to a halt, shielding his face from the flying glass. There was no way to tell who it was and in any case his attention was taken by the huge, unharmed, black wolf straddling the corpse.

28

Towner opened fire, but he was too slow. The woman and the wolf were gone. He ran after her, shouting for help. His heavy boots pounded on the concrete as he sprinted, but she was much, much faster than him and disappeared into the darkness of the urine drenched stairwell.

29

Miller curled into a ball when he saw the wolf and stayed that way as Towner started shooting. He heard Towner's shouts but couldn't move. His limbs were locked around his shaking body, and he wasn't going anywhere.

Hands on his shoulders pulled him back to the moment. He looked into Penfold's concerned face.

"Come on, man," she said. "They're getting away."

He shook his head, shame biting deep inside him. *Training. All that training. Jesus, that wolf was huge. All those teeth and claws....*

"Get your arse up." Penfold's voice was gentle, despite the situation. "We gotta go, we gotta go, now!"

Miller nodded and let her drag him to his feet. He picked his SA80 up, its weight comforting in his arms.

"You okay?"

He nodded again but didn't trust speaking. Bursting into tears right now would not be a good look. *I'm not sure I'm ever going to be okay again.*

"Follow me."

Penfold headed for the stairwell, running after Towner and the woman. With great reluctance, Miller followed.

30

The wolf crept off the car, its movements slow and deliberate, head low but not taking its eyes off Knowles. It was still around ten metres from him, roughly halfway between him and the two members of Bravo still at the stairwell. The other two had run after the family.

Knowles had been here before, staring down a wolf, not quite sure how it was going to go. Of course, there was the shit-show in Exeter too, but, Christ, as bad as that had been, there was something bowel-loosening about looking at this unnatural thing. Knowles didn't subscribe to the current feeling that *all* wolves were evil, but dammit, most of them were.

He tensed, ready to raise his weapon.

The wolf prowled closer.

31

Harry still hurt from landing on the car. The soldier had helped break his fall, true, but he'd still hit the car roof with some force. If he hadn't changed, he would have definitely broken something.

The soldier in front of him didn't seem too scared, which was a first for Harry. Most humans shat themselves when they saw a wolf in the flesh. Not this guy. Maybe that would make him taste better.

32

The wolf looked ready to pounce. Knowles raised his weapon, aiming down the sights in one smooth practised action.

And for the second time in five minutes, everything went wrong.

Another wolf leapt out of the stairwell, smashing through the two Bravo team members, sending them crashing to the floor. It howled, and the other wolf turned its head to watch.

Knowles squeezed the trigger.

A third wolf hit him from the side, sending his bullets wild as he fell. Knowles rolled quickly, keeping a tight grip on his weapon. Heart thumping, adrenaline surging, he came up to a kneeling stance, but both wolves were running away from him, dodging through the car park. The third was still outside the door, biting into a Bravo member. He fired but missed both of the fleeing wolves.

33

Towner emerged into the chaos just as a third wolf sent Knowles flying. The woman he'd chased had changed also, somewhere on the stairwell.

He stopped.

Weapon braced to his shoulder.

Feet shoulder width apart, keeping his aim steady.

Breathe in.

Fire.

Bullets tore into the wolf, ripping its flesh apart and sending it tumbling to the tarmac. It twitched, trying to get back to its feet. Towner smelled cordite and the fetid odour of the beast in front him. It stared at him, eyes full of pain, fear and rage.

He shot it in the head, of course.

34

Harry staggered, stopping as he heard the shots ring out. Somehow, by zigzagging, he'd evaded all the other soldier's shots. He hadn't been scared at all, that soldier, which unnerved Harry.

He looked back, trying to get a better look at the man, but his attention was dragged left, towards the doorway. Flo hit the ground.

Saw the soldier shoot her at point blank range.

Saw her head explode, her brain splashing over the concrete behind.

Harry felt like he'd been smacked in the stomach with a sledge-hammer. Air rushed out of him, and he collapsed, turning back into a human before he hit the ground. The tarmac was cool under his bare skin, and he heaved and retched but nothing came out.

"Flo!" he screamed.

Harry could still see the soldier, who was toeing Flo like she was roadkill. He lifted her head with his boot and let it fall back to the concrete. Harry could cover that distance in a second. Rip his throat out and feast on his innards until the sun came up tomorrow.

Chris grabbed his arm. "No man. We need to go, or they get us all."

Harry looked at the hand holding him, then back at the soldier. Chris was a lot bigger than him, and he held fast. Chris, who had come back to help Harry and Flo, but only half succeeded.

Chris's face softened; the first time Harry had seen any sort of emotion on either brothers' face. "No sense you dying too."

A car pulled up at the head of the street, an overweight man driving, with an equally overweight woman in the passenger seat. Rich opened the rear door and beckoned to them.

Chris pulled on Harry's arm once more. "Don't be stupid," he said, but let go and ran for the sanctity of the car. Harry glared at the soldier for a second longer, then turned and ran after Chris.

35

Knowles heard a car screech away from the head of the road but didn't see it. He sprinted down the street, passing the two dead Bravo members, but by the time he got to the junction with the main road, it was long gone.

CHAPTER 2

1

Harry got out of the car as soon as it stopped. During the drive, cool air had become cold, and he shivered. He rested a hand on the car roof and threw up before sinking to his knees. Tears spilled down his face, and he wiped at his eyes, trying and failing to get rid of them. His hands shook and he felt like every limb was floating and weak at the same time.

Shock. You're in shock. Get a grip.

The other car doors opened, spilling all occupants out onto the verge. A bridge loomed above them, down a side road off the A-road that was essentially a dirt track. Harry had no idea where they were, except outside North London and a long way from the flats.

The overweight couple clutched each other, fear easy to see (and smell) in the headlights. Harry glanced at them, but sensing their panic only brought more bile up. *Flo. Jesus, help me. Flo. What will I do without you?* He could rip them apart in seconds, but it wouldn't bring her back, wouldn't help anything.

"Please don't hurt us," the woman screeched. Essex accent, highlighted by her fear.

"Shut the fuck up," Rich said. He was the only wolf with clothes on.

"Up you get, mate." Chris said, not unkindly, and he helped Harry stand. He didn't seem bothered by the cold. He offered a tissue from a box in the back of the car. Harry took it, with a weak smile, and wiped his mouth.

Flo.

"Just let us go," the man said. "We won't say nothing." The pathetic whine in his voice set Harry's teeth on edge. He could almost see Flo shaking her head in his mind.

Chris was in his face in an instant, shoulders square and muscles tense. "You won't be able to if I rip your throat out."

The man started shaking, and the woman held him tighter. Hours before they'd been at each other's throats, audible over the blare of their pointless tv shows. *Amazing what a bit of genuine fear will do to sharpen your mind.*

"Back up, Chris, we need to think." Harry could picture Flo, smiling at his words.

"What's to think about?" Rich leaned on the other side of the car. He looked so relaxed he could be ordering a pint in a pub. "They've seen us."

The woman wailed.

"If you kill them, we become what they think we are." Harry's mouth was full of acid bile, and it took every ounce of his willpower not to take a bite to wash away the taste. Every thought was centred on Flo and what she would do.

"They already think we're animals," Rich said. His voice was soft, letting the words have all the power. "They are hunting us."

Chris nodded, agreeing with his brother as he always did. Was he even capable of independent thought? "No-one will even miss these fat pricks."

"We have a son!" The man had stopped shaking. He looked angry now. *Ah, the fight part.*

"I don't give a shit," Chris said.

"Calm down," Harry said. "We don't need to do anything stupid here."

"You calling my brother stupid?" Rich, still calm.

"Yeah, you calling me stupid?" Chris turned to face Harry, the other two forgotten for a moment.

Harry sighed and held his hand up. "No, I most definitely am not. Look, we just got our arses kicked. Flo—" his voice hitched, "—Flo is dead. The others too. Now is not the time to fight amongst ourselves."

Rich smirked. "Relax Harry, we're all on the same side, remember."

"Yeah, same side."

Harry tried not to let his frustration show. Instead, he advanced on the couple. The man's anger faded and his eyes opened wide. His nostrils flared. Harry saw himself through the man's terrified gaze. Naked. Well-muscled. Covered in blood – crucially, other people's blood. He held up a hand, palm out. "Do you know what just happened?"

"You came into our home and fucking kidnapped us," the woman blurted. "Made us help you. We did that. Just let us go." Her husband looked to the stars, and Harry had a sense of how her forthrightness might be wearing.

"We saved ourselves," he said with as much patience as he could muster. "Did what we had to do. None of us asked for this. None of us wants to be hunted. We just want to live in peace."

"You eat people!"

"Steph—"

Harry snorted. "Not all of us. There are as many different types of us as there are you. We don't all eat people." He gestured at Chris and Rich. "We don't."

Rich grinned in a way that left them in doubt that whatever Harry said, *he* just might.

"My wife just got shot by soldiers on British streets. Does that seem right to you? No trial. No 'innocent before proven guilty'. No chance to defend herself against crimes she has not committed. Just BANG and game over."

The man flinched.

"Does that seem right to you?" Harry repeated, jabbing the man in the chest. Anger was helping keep the cold away.

"But—"

"Does it? We're being hunted in our own land and we. Haven't. Done. Anything. Wrong." A jab on each word, getting harder each time.

"Tell him, Harry," Rich said. He was enjoying himself a bit too much for Harry's liking.

"Yeah, tell him."

"Those soldiers don't answer to anyone. They can do what they like. Shoot to kill, no questions asked. It's not right."

"Damn straight it's not right."

Harry shot a glance at Rich, relieved to have him back onside. "I need you to go to the press. Tell them what you've seen tonight. Tell them innocent, harmless people are being killed by our own soldiers. Tell them a man lost his wife just because she is different and then ask people if they think that's right."

He was breathing hard. Could feel his limbs trembling. His head pounded like a drum, and every time he blinked, he saw flashes of Flo. Her smile. Her eyes. Her smile. God, her smile. Interspersed with the happy images: her bleeding outside a dingy block of flats; her eyes rolling back in her head as heroin bit deeper and deeper; her weariness at being on the run for so long.

"I'm tired," Harry said, even though he felt anything but that. "I'm so, so tired. I've been on the run for so long, I can't remember what it's like to have an address." He paused, then snarled at the man. "I can't remember the shittiness of bills. Of arguing over what to watch on the TV. Of going to work. Of *stability* and boredom. Can you imagine that?" He snorted. "I miss the boredom of going to work."

The man had the sense to shake his head, but then he said something so monumentally stupid, Harry nearly tore his throat out.

"So are you like vegetarian wolves or something?"

"Davey," Steph said, panic clear in her voice.

Rich started laughing, so of course, Chris joined in. "Vegetarian wolves? That's a good one."

Harry didn't crack a smile. Instead, he took a step closer to the man. There was less distance between them than between lovers. "Am I a joke to you?"

Davey, already pale but getting paler by the second, shook his head. "No. No. No. Sorry. I didn't mean anything. I didn't think."

"My wife died today. I am looking for an excuse to take my anger out on something. Some*one*. Do you want that to be you?"

Davey continued shaking his head, but now with such force, small drops of saliva splashed out of his mouth.

"Kill him," Rich said. He still leant on the roof of the car, looking more relaxed than ever before. He could have been ordering a pizza.

"Yeah, fucking end him."

Harry kept close to Davey for another heartbeat, a moment that stretched and stretched. He could feel the wolf inside, itching to come out and play. The man was overweight enough to be several meals and his wife—

Harry took a step back, then another. With the second, his legs buckled for a moment, and he stumbled. Cold air bit at him again, reminding him of his lack of clothing.

"I want your clothes," he said.

"And your motorcycle." Rich laughed. Chris joined in again, but he looked confused, clearly not getting the reference.

Davey stared at Harry, his mouth dropping open. "They won't fit you," he managed at last.

"Better than nothing. Get naked, fat man." Harry knew he should be ashamed of himself for that barb and hell, Flo would have torn a strip off him – not literally of course.

"Do it, Davey," Steph said, eyeing up Chris as she did. Her eyes travelled over his taut flesh, lingering on his muscles and skirting over the scars.

Davey frowned, and for a moment Harry thought he would burst into tears.

"I'm not going to hurt you," Harry said with a sigh. "I'm just cold."

Davey moved with a speed that belied his size, stripping down to his boxers in seconds. Yellow stains dotted the front. He started to pull them down, but Harry held up a hand.

"I'm good, I'll go commando." Harry pulled on the clothes – a filthy shirt, wife beater vest and baggy jeans. They hung off him like a kid playing dress up. He didn't care.

"What am I going to do now?" Davey said, goosebumps clear on his arms as he hugged himself.

"Go away, before I change my mind."

Davey looked around, peering back down the lane. Darkness was rapidly falling all around them. Steph held on to her husband, no longer eyeing Chris up.

"Run away, you thick fuck." Rich stood to his full height for the first time, the threat unmistakeable.

"Yeah, run, lard arse."

Davey started to run back down the lane, Steph close behind.

"We should kill him, you know," Rich said.

"Yeah, put him out of his misery."

Harry shook his head. "No, then we become what they say we are."

"Is that a bad thing?" Rich said.

Harry didn't bother to answer, but just got in the car. Chris and Rich clambered in after him, Chris sliding into the back seat without a comment.

Harry drummed his fingers on the steering wheel. How had the day turned to such shit? Not even two hours ago, they'd been sat in a warm, although admittedly filthy, flat, surrounded by friends and his wife had been alive. Now what?

"You got a plan?" Rich said.

"I could use some clothes." Chris smiled as he spoke. Harry wasn't sure he'd ever met anyone as comfortable in their own skin as Chris.

"Scotland," Harry said.

"What the fuck?" Chris said.

Harry looked at Rich. The other man seemed content to go along with whatever Harry said. For now.

"Gary spoke about someone who bit him in Scotland. Healed him of cancer. That sound like anyone you've heard of?"

Rich sneered at him. "Bollocks. If that guy ever existed, he'd be dead by now surely?"

"It's worth a look. You got a better idea?"

He hadn't.

2

They were in the car barely a minute when Rich said, "Hold up, I need a piss."

"Really?" Harry said. "It'd be better to have a few more miles between us first."

"When you gotta go, you gotta go."

Harry pulled over, still grumbling to himself. They weren't even back on the main road yet, but on the service track for the bridge.

"Be quick," Harry said.

"Oh, I will be."

3

Steph was crying as they walked. The cold bit deep into her, and Davey moaned as he walked.

"I'm fucking freezing. That was my best shirt what he took then. Skinny bastard."

"At least we're alive," she said. Some days, most if she were honest with herself, she hated her husband. Hated their lives. Hated sitting in that flat, watching pennies until the next benefits payment hit. She could get a job, maybe that would alleviate the boredom. Yeah, work for someone else, just to get the same as she got now? Fuck that. They'd been married eight years and had fought every day of those eight (and a fair few before then), but she'd never hit him, and he'd never laid a finger on her either. Their sparring had always been verbal. She knew that wasn't true for some of their neighbours.

Something moved behind Davey.

Something big.

"Steph?"

She didn't respond. Couldn't in fact, speak or move a muscle as terror overwhelmed her. Davey started to turn, slowly, because he knew what was behind him, and knew it was all over before he finished the turn.

4

Rich got back into the car, wiping his mouth with the back of his hand. "Sorry lads, needed a dump."

"Jesus, you've been ages," Harry said. "Fuck's sake, Rich, we need to be gone from here."

"He said he was sorry," Chris said. "Got to drop the kids off at the pool when you got to."

Harry shook his head. *I'm travelling with imbeciles.* "Where can we lay low?"

"We're not laying low," Rich said. "Get us North, Harry. We're going to Scotland. Like you said, there's someone we need to have a wee chat with."

Chris sniggered, and Harry guessed it was because his brother had said 'wee'.

"Okay," Harry said. "Good idea."

Rich held his stare, eyes boring into him. "Harry, you seem to be thinking I give a fuck about your opinion. You also seem to be thinking you call the shots around here."

Chris laughed again, the stupid braying noise irritating Harry more than the Essex accents. "North we go, lads, eh? Give it an hour, yeah, then can we get something to eat?"

"Nah, not hungry." Rich said with a smirk. "Get us going, Harry."

CHAPTER 3

1

Knowles surveyed the chaos with an all too familiar sick feeling in his stomach. How many times had he seen an encounter with wolves end like this? Paramedics swarmed the stairwell, checking everyone out, making sure no-one was hurt. Towner and Penfold watched closely as the residents of the block filed past, hoping their presence alone would flush some wolves out. Knowles hid a smirk at the though. Most residents had argued as soon as the call to evacuate the building came, but sight of the dead wolf in the car park and the heavily armed soldiers soon put a stop to the protests.

Police maintained a cordon at a distance. He could see them, leaning on their vehicles in their high viz, drinking coffee from flasks. He envied them, as they laughed and joked. Maybe he could be a cop when he left the military. That'd be alright, and nowhere near as dangerous as what he did now. How hard could it be, sitting in a car and arresting drunks?

Knowles snorted, knowing he was being ridiculous. If there was a league of most misunderstood jobs, military had to be number one, with the police close behind. Teachers or maybe nurses coming in third.

What the hell is wrong with you?

It wasn't the first time that thought had crossed his mind. He was freewheeling, thinking about anything and everything but the shit show in front of him. *What a mess.*

A white van pulled up, with a camera crew disembarking almost before it had stopped moving. Knowles groaned and waved at one of the police officers. She frowned at him as he pointed at the van, but then understood. Pulling a cap on, she walked over to the press, sticking a hand in front of the camera. Knowles could see them arguing even from this distance.

Get them the fuck away from here. No-one wants to see this in their living rooms.

His job had become harder and harder since knowledge of the wolves reached the public around ten years ago. There had been rumours for decades, lots of sightings, but nothing concrete until a crew ripped apart a service station in Kent. A teenage girl filmed it all and her body was found outside, where she'd made a run for it. She'd nearly escaped. Her photo had become the very human face of the threat posed by wolves. As soon as the mangled photos of her body turned up online, any pretence these things didn't exist had to stop. Kind of hard to keep that quiet or covered up.

The motorway services had been an utter blood bath, but he'd only seen pictures of it. He'd chased the pack across the country to a small village in Devon. Huntleigh. Him and Stadler. *A lifetime ago.*

Since then, he'd been in charge of the nation's response to the 'wolf problem'. He'd established a team – a good one too – and then the cluster fuck of Exeter had happened. He couldn't blame the wolves for that. Exeter had been something worse, which he hadn't even thought possible. That particular shitshow removed wolves from the front pages, and the wolf deniers grew at an exponential rate. Knowles was never sure if the conspiracy theorists were a good or bad thing.

So here he was, back with a new team, chasing down wolves again, with that team already minus one member. Had he become complacent? Had he been underestimating the threat? Was it time to call it a day and finally retire?

The intel had been three in a flat. They'd known it was more before going in, and yet they still had two corpses inside, one on the balcony and one at the bottom of the stairwell. That was just the wolves – he had suffered his own losses. Three Bravo team, who, to his shame, he couldn't name, and Rawson.

And some wolves had escaped. All the audio was already back in Kent, being analysed for different voices. They wouldn't stop there. Voices would be stripped from the recordings, leaving them with breathing to help double check the body count. *Modern technology. What a time to be alive.* Until he had confirmation, he would assume a pack was on the loose.

Police were pulling the CCTV for the surrounding streets, but it was hard going. Lots of the cameras were smashed long before today, or had just stopped working. Maybe they'd get lucky, but they probably wouldn't.

Footsteps made him look up. Miller saluted, grimacing. His field dressing had been replaced with much neater stiches, and whilst the wound didn't look quite as angry as it had when he'd emerged from the stairwell earlier, he would never be considered handsome again.

"Miller. How're you feeling?"

Miller couldn't make eye contact, instead staring at a point just past Knowles' ear. He was one of those you see in school who tells anyone who would listen all they want to do is serve.

Serve.

Jesus wept. Why does no-one ever say what it actually is? Fighting. Controlled aggression – most of the time, barely controlled. Unimaginable terror punctuating the utter tedium.

"I let you down, sir."

That stopped his train of thought, and Knowles stood a little straighter. "How so?"

"I froze, sir." Miller finally met Knowles' gaze and his eyes were full of water. "I didn't react quick enough to the threat."

"React?" Knowles said, then laughed. "You just came face to face with something unnatural. Something that exists *just* to end you. All so it can eat."

"Sir, I—"

"Listen," Knowles said, keeping his voice low and even. "I've been dealing with this a lot longer than you, and every time I see one of those things, I just about shit myself. You're alive, that's one up on that poor bastard." Knowles pointed at Rawson, who was being carefully lifted off the car roof. A body bag sat on a nearby gurney. Even though he'd been told it was Rawson, he still couldn't quite believe it: nothing recognisable remained.

Miller still looked like he might cry and being reminded of Rawson's fate exacerbated that.

"Rawson did what he could. You did what you could. You'll be better prepared next time."

"Sir, if I'd reacted better then maybe Rawson would still be alive."

Knowles nodded. "Maybe. Maybe not. Maybe all you'd have done is piss it off and it would have killed you too. And Towner. And Penfold." Knowles needed a drink, badly. "You can't think about maybes. You just can't. How many tours have you done?"

He knew the answer already, but still needed to make the point.

"None, sir. I wanted to join your unit sir."

"Exactly. Do you know I veto everyone on this team?"

Miller shook his head with enough vigour to make Knowles worry for the security of the stitches in his face.

"I chose you. I agreed to have you on this team. Why do you think that is?"

Miller returned to staring past Knowles' ear. "I couldn't say, sir."

"Your scores in training were fantastic. Your shooting was one of the highest, repeatedly. You're a team player, too." Knowles smiled. "*That's* the sort of person I want. Someone I can work with. Trust. You won't freeze next time."

"But—" Miller definitely had tears in his eyes. "—what if I do?"

Knowles nodded softly. "Well, then you'll be being scraped into a body bag, and I'll be visiting your parents. Either way, you won't care."

Miller swallowed, any remaining colour draining from his face.

Knowles knew he was being harsh, but the kid needed reality right now, not empty *it'll be okay* platitudes.

"Go help Towner and Penfold," he said. "I don't think we've got any more surprises here tonight, but it doesn't hurt to be prepared."

Miller saluted again and ran to the stairwell.

Knowles sighed. Time to inspect the flat.

2

The flat was a mess, and not just because of the two corpses. One male, one female. According to Towner, he'd rolled a G60 grenade in, then opened fire. His report stated he was in control at all times, but the bullet holes in the wall and ripped apart sofa told a different story. White tufts of the sofa's insides lay strewn across the carpet.

The woman had been shot twice: one in the chest, one in the head. Either would have been the kill shot. The man seemed to have caught the full force of the flashbang. His left leg was a bloody, pulpy mess but he also had at least three bullet holes as far as Knowles could see.

He was lying in the doorway to a kitchen which had seen better days. Dishes covered every surface, most of them covered in dried food and a not inconsiderable amount of mould. Knowles counted one bong, three syringes and a rubber tube. *How do people live like this?*

He stepped over the man, into the kitchen and opened some cupboards. Tinned food in one, a solitary packet of Hobnobs in another and no sign of anything fresh or wholesome like fruit or vegetables. Knowles took one of the biscuits and grimaced at how soft it felt.

"For fuck's sake," he said.

"Captain?" Penfold had been in the bedroom, but she came as soon as he spoke.

"Who lets Hobnobs go stale? Jesus, what a waste."

Penfold's face said she didn't know if he was joking or not, but also that she didn't think jokes were appropriate. Knowles sighed. Some people had no sense of humour. *She'd learn. When the shit hits the fan, bad jokes are all we have left.*

"Look at the state of this place."

Penfold nodded, relieved to not be part of any more inappropriate banter. "It's the drugs, sir."

Well, no shit, Sherlock.

"Yeah, the drugs. If it looks like a duck, or..." He waved a hand like there was more to come.

"Sorry sir?"

"Never mind."

He squeezed through the narrow gap between her bulk and the door, heading into the bedroom. This had probably been the only clean room in the house originally, but now a fine layer of plaster dust settled on the dresser and the mattress. No doubt on the top of the wardrobe too.

A large hole wrecked the wall above the bed, leading through into the flat next door. He inspected it, realising the walls were paper thin and so anyone could have made the hole, not just wolves. There was still no sign of the occupants of the flat. An Alex and Steph Snell. Their car was missing too, police searching for it via security cameras and ANC. Nothing yet.

"What'll the police do now?"

He turned to Penfold. She leant in the doorway, arms folded. "Not much they can do. We have total control of this scene. They work for us, not the other way round. Most police I've met want nothing to do with the wolves. They'll control a news blackout; we'll take care of the rest. If they find our missing wolves, they'll contact us before they do anything stupid like engage."

"Understood, sir." She looked like she was going to say more, but kept her mouth shut.

"Spill it, Penfold."

She wrestled with it for a few seconds, the silence between them stretching until Knowles thought it would become permanent.

"Miller, sir."

Here we go.

"Is he okay, sir?"

"He'll be fine."

She nodded. "Good. It was scary sir. I've never seen anything like it."

Well, that's a surprise.

"You'll get used to it."

"I'm not sure I want to." She smiled but her eyes were dark. "Miller's a good guy, sir. Are you going to can him?"

Knowles failed to hide his surprise at the directness of the question. *Young recruits these days. No way I would have spoken to my Captain like that.* He scanned the room, reluctant to touch anything – not to preserve the scene, but because it all looked so disgusting.

"No."

Penfold got the message and made herself busy looking around the right side of the bed. A bedside table that was small enough to be an insult to other bedside tables held a book and an empty glass. She picked up the glass and sniffed it before she really thought about what she was doing.

Knowles grinned as she blanched.

"Fuck knows what was in there, sir, but there's no way I'd have drunk it." She pulled open the tiny drawer in the table, revealing a black leather pouch. "Sir," she said.

"What's in it?"

She opened the pouch, unrolling it slowly. It held syringes, all clean and unused. They were tucked neatly into individual slots stitched into the leather. This was something they'd seen on their last raid. Then, the wolves had been long gone, but they'd left in a hurry, and Knowles recovered a lot of drug paraphernalia.

"More drugs, sir."

He didn't correct her. "Wonder why they're shooting up so much."

"Desperation," she said. "Used to see it on the estates back home." She shrugged, turning away from his enquiring stare. "I got out, sir, that's all that matters."

Knowles didn't want to push her any further. "What's the book?"

Penfold picked up the volume, looking like she'd seen it for the first time. "Something called *The Finite.*" She read the spine and back blurb. "Kit Power. Never heard of him. Sounds bleak as fuck."

"Let's see," Knowles said, holding his hands up. She threw it to him, and something flew out from between the pages. It spun in the air, landing on the bed. A postcard, creased and scuffed: like the rest of the flat, it had clearly seen better days.

Penfold scooped it up, holding it close to inspect it. It showed some buildings surrounded by trees – clearly an aerial shot. In one corner it said, 'Charity of the year' and in another 'The Losthorn Village'.

"Losthorn. Where's that?"

Knowles snatched the postcard from her, checking the back out, but it was blank, nothing written there.

"You alright, sir? You've gone a bit pale."

If she was put out at him snatching the postcard, she wasn't showing it.

"Yeah fine."

"You heard of this place then?"

Knowles paused, just a fraction of a second too long. He tugged at his earlobe. "No. Never heard of it. We'll Google maps it, yeah?" He stuffed the postcard into a pocket. "Come on, we're about done here. Let's let the local police have a go, and then I want the disposal team in."

"Sir." Penfold followed him out of the flat, and Knowles knew from the expression on her face that she'd clocked his lie. Nothing was ever easy when you were dealing with wolves.

3

Knowles sat on the bonnet of their truck, drinking lukewarm, awful coffee and tapping the postcard on his leg. Penfold, Miller and Towner were joking near the local police, but not engaging with them beyond the odd nod or thanks for the coffee. Given one of the team had died, they seemed in good spirits. A depleted Bravo team had already returned to base, replaced by the disposal team. He guessed the decapitation and burning of the wolves' corpses would not be suitable viewing for the ten o'clock news.

Knowles looked again at the postcard. The Losthorn Village. *Shit.*

He slung the dregs of his cup into the verge alongside him. It was a pathetic strip of grass, although there was definitely more mud than greenery there. Maybe the coffee would help the grass grow. Maybe not.

Knowles took out his mobile and scrolled through his contacts. He kept an eye on his team, making sure they were at a distance. Making sure they couldn't hear him.

He selected a number; one he hadn't used for a few years now. *BC.* He hadn't even put the guy's full name in, just initials. The team were still on the other side of the car park, still chatting. Knowles took a deep breath and pressed call.

Surprised at how nervous he felt, he waited for the call to connect. What would he do if it was answered? What would he do if it was out of service? After what felt like an age where Knowles sprouted a few more grey hairs, he heard the click of the call going through.

Answerphone. A bland one, an automated female voice announcing the phone number, then the beep.

"It's me," he said. "I found something today, something that might link to your neck of the woods. Be alert, trouble could be coming your way. Maybe not, and I'm really hoping not, but be vigilant and call if you see anything out of place."

He hung up, slipping the phone back into his tunic. Then he banged the side of the truck. "Wheels up folks, let's get out of here."

Interlude – Huntleigh

3 months earlier

1

Alex Thorne ran. Headphones in so he could listen to music, but also so he could hear the beeps to help maintain his pace. Huntleigh was a bit shit – middle of nowhere, although full of nice people, only two pubs and a church that had seen better days – so keeping fit remained a way to fill his days.

Of course, the sarge would bollock him if he let his standards go, but Alex wasn't too worried about her: definitely had a bark worse than her bite. Besides, what exactly could she do to him? They had another eight months to go on this placement, or more precisely, thirty-nine weeks and three days. Potter, his roommate, had it counted on a calendar, even though he'd signed up for repeat rounds. Alex couldn't blame him – the place sucked, yes, but at least no-one was shooting at them.

However, sitting in a village in Devon was not what Alex had signed up for, despite what Captain Knowles said about it being a vital part of the mission. *Utter bollocks.*

His feet pounded the roads, because Huntleigh had very few pavements. *What the fuck is that all about?* He ran along a road between houses. One side looked new, like they'd been built in the last twenty years, the other in the last two hundred. The road wasn't wide enough for two cars to pass, so he wasn't worried about having his music loud as he ran.

Mental checkpoints rattled through his head. There, on the left, the small house belonging to the local vicar. Another hundred metres, then also on the left, the larger, but still small, house with constantly closed curtains. Maybe they'd be open later, but he'd never seen it. He had no idea how the owners made money as they never seemed to leave the house. His route turned uphill, taking him past the primary school. Maybe he should change the time of his run, come past at about eight thirty instead, see some young mums. He chuckled to himself – now that *would* get him in trouble with the sarge.

The locals called this 'cardiac hill' and he felt his legs and chest burn – a good burn, meant he was working hard – as he reached the summit. Here the road turned back into the village or continued up a gentler slope to another small estate on the outskirts. He jogged through this estate which, being new, held the younger families of Huntleigh. One bloke was out at his car as Alex jogged past, and the man gave him a 'Morning' that was way too cheery. His wife stood in the doorway, looking tired as she waved her husband goodbye. She closed the door before Alex could really take in her silky night dress, but he wasn't interested anyway. *Too old for me. She's, like, forty at least.*

Alex passed through and turned back into the village square. Here was the shop, the vets and, of course, the two pubs. He ran past both, circled back down past a garage, and then turned into the street where they were billeted.

The route was a mile, and he ran the circuit three times. On his third round, more cars had left drives, the garage was open and the pubs were taking deliveries. Another van blocked the road by the shop, with a couple of young men ferrying big trays of bread inside.

This was Huntleigh. This was his route. Same thing every day. Alex had seen enough in the short time he'd been here to know that civvy street was not for him. *Nope, a life in the service with a juicy pension and then feet up on a beach. Or maybe a ski resort. Whatever, not that nine to five shit.* Even so, it felt good to be out and about. Felt good to do something other than stare at a screen.

Alex had been in Huntleigh for ten days and he was already bored.

2

Alex stopped dead in his tracks. *Who the hell is that?*

Today he'd left the village and gone down the hill, towards the Ploughmans' house. A different route, but one Potter had suggested. Alex welcomed it – running around the village had become so boring after a while, and he'd repeated it for around three weeks already. Potter said to run up into the woods, get a change of scene, so that's what he'd done for the last week.

His new route took him out of their house – laughably called a safe house, but in reality, it was no more secure than any other in Huntleigh – and down the hill, away from the village. Every time he ran past the house Jack Stadler had lived in, goosebumps broke out along his arms. *So much death caused by that man.*

The Ploughmans lived at the bottom of the hill, in an enormous house set back from the road. A permissive path cut across their land, leading up into the woods where everything had all started, many years ago. *To think nobody had even suspected the wolves were real until then.* He wasn't sure he even believed it, but he'd read the files, seen the footage. Only a fool would discount evidence like that, although the internet was full of such people.

Alex took the permissive path, and that's when he saw *her*.

The most beautiful woman he had ever seen emerged from a red Mini Cooper parked on the drive. She was wearing jeans and a big, fluffy white coat, hair in a loose knot at the back of her head and no make-up. He tried not to gawp as she slammed the car door shut and hefted a pink day bag onto her shoulder. Every movement was graceful, and she smiled as she saw him, raising a hand in greeting.

He lost his footing and staggered, but kept running, even though his heart beat a little faster and all he wanted to do was stop. She turned away from him, now waving at someone coming out the gate.

Ploughman, senior. Emilia. She had dark hair cut to a bob, giving her a harsher look than she perhaps deserved. The woman ran to her, throwing her arms around her neck and shouting "Mum!".

"Jordan." Emilia returned the hug, but the whole time her eyes were on Alex.

And then they were out of view as Alex ran along the path and into the woods. As he ran, his mind kept flashing back to the raised hand only now it added a wry smile. Each time the smile got a little wider, her eyes a little sexier.

He shook his head. He'd always been a fan of women who understated their beauty. No need for loads of makeup or skimpy clothes. Alex wondered if she was single. How long was she in Huntleigh for, and, most important of all, what was she doing later?

Alex grinned to himself and upped his pace. He knew exactly how to find that out.

3

Back at the house, showered and two mugs of tea made, Alex went to see the sarge. She sat in the smallest room in the house: upstairs, middle bedroom, essentially large enough to host a single bed. Instead, it held a four-by-four array of monitors covered one wall; recording equipment lined another and two chairs sat by the desk beneath the monitors, which displayed live images from around the village and nearby woods.

The cameras covered all angles of the woods, focussed around where Jack Stadler had fallen. The hole wasn't there anymore – filled in by Captain Knowles when he'd blown the whole thing up – and they didn't want to risk anyone falling in again. Other cameras covered both pubs, just so they could monitor local conversations. The final set was installed in the Ploughmans' house. It was the closest house in the village to the underground cave system where the bones were. In fact, from their pantry, there was only about ten feet of rock between the rear wall and the start of the caves, according to satellite imagery.

Back when he'd first been interviewed for this team, he'd asked why they needed a team there. Surely the bones were inaccessible? No-one was getting near them without heavy duty digging equipment. Captain Knowles had agreed with him, but he needed to be sure. *Healthy paranoia* was how he described it. Alex still had his doubts, but kept quiet. Who was he to say what the boss spent tax payers money on? This beat the shit out of another tour somewhere hot where you never knew who was friend or foe.

"Brew, Sarge," he said, putting the mug in front of her.

Rachel Kenny smiled at him and nodded in gratitude. "Cheers, Al."

He winced, but if she noticed she didn't say anything. "Wasson?" Alex gave a perfect imitation of the local Devonian accent. The phrase had made him chuckle at first, as had many of the other local expressions. *Where's it to? Proper job. I'll be there dreckly. Maid. Bey. Cream first.*

Most of those were said by the older folk in the village but it always made Alex do a double take when he heard younger people speak like that. His first few shifts on the monitors had made him cry with laughter – the way they spoke down here was too funny. *They'd say the same about you.* He knew that – you could take the boy out of Essex and all that.

The others didn't really share his humour. They were alright, and up for a laugh, but they couldn't see why he found the way the locals spoke so funny. Six of them shared the op in total, so two were always on duty. Right now, it was just him and the Sarge.

Sandeman was God knows where. She would always shoot off in her car as soon as her turn was over. Alex wasn't sure how the sarge put up with that, but then Sandeman had been doing this op the longest: nearly two years now.

Wijnberg and Howells were off together, as always. They were asleep in the main bedroom, no doubt with bunks pushed together. Again, the sarge turned a blind eye – as long as they did their job, who cared if they bunked up together?

The final member of their team, Potter, spent his downtime in the pub, mixing with the locals. The sarge encouraged this, always saying knowing the locals would help to identify if something was up. Alex wondered if anything was going on between the two of them, but Potter just laughed when he asked.

Alex pulled the headphones on and cycled through all the feeds. The bank of screens included a larger one at eye level, so they could zoom in on any one image. He pulled this up and saw the Ploughmans' kitchen.

It was larger than his entire flat back at the base. Dominated by a large island in the middle, it had cupboards around the outside and a massive American style fridge in the corner. They had two cookers –an Aga and a normal electric one. The other half of the room contained a large dining table. It was the sort of room Alex aspired to owning at some point in the future, whilst acknowledging his army salary and pension wouldn't ever allow him to.

Emilia and Jordan were sat at the table. He pulled on headphones and switched the audio feed on.

"—she'll come around."

Jordan pulled a face. Even with the fisheye lens, she took Alex's breath away. "I've never seen anyone so angry, Mum."

"It's not every day your favourite student drops out of college."

"I hated it. I told you – and *her* – that."

"I said you didn't need a MA," Emilia said.

"I know, I know, but I wanted it." A pause. "I thought I wanted it. Everyone on the course was so stuck up though, and pretentious. Twats, the lot of them."

Emilia pulled a face. "Don't speak like that. You're not a sailor."

Jordan laughed, a sound Alex would pay money to hear over and over. "Mum, I'm twenty-two, I can say what I want."

"Not in this house."

She waved a hand at her but didn't repeat the swearing.

"So what are you going to do now?" Emilia broke the silence.

"Long term, no clue. I need to look around, see what my options are. Short term, the Kings might give me my old job back."

Emilia smiled, but it was awkward, like she wasn't used to the action. "They love you up there. Always asking about you."

"I'll head up there in a while. Tea?"

Alex took the headphones off as she stood and put the kettle on. So, Jordan was going to the pub shortly. He knew what he was doing with the rest of the day.

4

Jordan was already behind the bar when he walked into the pub. Potter was, of course, already there, his hulking frame looking like it covered half the bar. It didn't, but still, Potter was a big bastard. Alex slid onto a stool next to him.

"Pint?"

Potter grunted and drained the remainder of his glass. Alex raised a hand at Jordan, earning a snort from Potter.

"Jordan, my mate wants your attention," Potter said. "Stick a pint in there." He gave her the glass and she pulled a pint from the Yellowhammer pump without saying a word to big man.

She put the glass in front of him then turned her radiance to Alex. "How about you?" This close, her eyes had a gleam, a mischievous glint which only highlighted the blue in them. Alex swallowed, his heart wanting to burst from his chest.

Jordan smirked. Clearly, she knew what affect she was having on him. "One of them?" She pointed at Potter.

Alex nodded, his mouth dry. In truth, he was afraid to talk. His voice would come out all high pitched and squeaky, she would laugh at him and that would be that.

Jordan put the full glass in front of him, then grinned. "There you go, *Alex.*"

Something about the way she said his name, the way she smiled at him, the curve of her lips, the way she brushed her hair away from her face, the way—

"For fuck's sake, Alex," Potter rolled his eyes. "Just pay the good lady and put your tongue away."

Alex felt heat rush to his cheeks, and he looked down at the bar even as he pressed his card to the reader.

"Want the receipt?"

He nodded and she pressed a piece of paper in his hand. The warmth of her touch sent sparks through him. She grinned again, then went to serve another customer.

"Cheers for that," Alex said, voice dripping with sarcasm.

"Any time, bro," Potter said with a smirk. "You got good taste though, I'll give you that. I would ruin that."

Alex cringed inside. Potter was late thirties, huge, bald, and had the sort of face even a mother would struggle with. Scars crossed his right cheek, darker stripes against his dark skin, a long-term reminder of an IED. Potter would not have been handsome without them, but with them, he was hard to look at.

"Who's on?" The big man spoke so quietly, Alex had to strain to hear him.

"Howells and Wijnberg," he said.

"They stopped fucking long enough to turn up on time? Bloody hell, Wijnberg is slipping."

Alex sipped his drink in lieu of an answer. The beer slipped down, warm, but tasty. Not lager, but then he'd always struggled with the chemicals in that.

"I'm going to make a move," Potter said, and for a horrible moment, Alex thought he meant on Jordan, but he drained his entire pint and stood. No wobble, no stagger. *Man, he can drink.* "Get some sleep before my shift. Later, mater."

He clapped a hand on Alex's shoulder, nearly sending him flying, burped loudly and left. Jordan finished serving and sauntered back towards Alex. He tried not to focus on the slow sway of her hips.

"He's a charmer, isn't he?"

"He's not so bad," Alex said.

"Old friend?"

"Yeah, we served together." Kenny had said that in any interaction with the locals, they should stay as close to the truth as possible without saying why they were there.

"Served? Past tense?"

She was sharp, this one.

"Yeah. He said he had some work down here and he needed some people."

"Oh yeah? Doing what?" She smiled. "Or would you have to kill me if you told me?"

He returned the smile. "Nah, nothing like that. We run security down on a couple of estates in Exeter. Easy money really."

"Even now?"

"Especially now. The rebuilding is going well, but the estates we manage are on the out-skirts, so they weren't touched by—" He paused, not really sure how to finish the sentence. Some of his mates had died in Exeter. Bawden and McLean. The ones who had recommended him to Knowles' unit just before, well, just before.

"It was awful, wasn't it?"

He drank more of his pint – not trusting his voice not to break.

"You new here?" he said instead.

"Yeah, first day again."

"Again?"

"I was a student, but I'm from here. Worked here every holiday to pay for uni."

"Not a student anymore? What are you going to do?"

"No clue yet. Get a proper job I suppose."

"You didn't do one of those arty degrees where you're basically unemployable did you?" The words were out before he really thought them through. *Fucking students.*

She laughed. "No, I'm an engineer, actually. Structural stuff."

"Not much call for that around here."

"You'd be surprised. There's plenty of work around with these old buildings, their roofs and foundations. Lots of foundation stuff underground." She smirked, lips turned into a sly grin and Alex's heart sped up again. "I need a bit of time out first though, recharge my batteries, you know?"

Alex nodded. *Yeah, we could all do with a bit of that.* He was surprised at how easy she was to talk to, how she seemed to be enjoying chatting with him. There were others sat near the bar, yet here she was, talking to him. This was going way better than he expected. He rubbed his hands on his jeans, wiping his suddenly clamming palms. *Ah fuck it.*

"So, um, what are you doing tomorrow?"

She smiled at him.

CHAPTER 4

Near Losthorn, Scotland

1

"Night, sir."

"Night Mr Bradshaw."

"See you tomorrow, sir."

"It's Saturday tomorrow, James. Not being funny, but I hope I don't see you then." Oliver Bradshaw smiled at the students as they filed out, still surprised at the thanks he was getting. It hadn't ever happened to him at any of his previous schools. James had the good sense to look embarrassed at forgetting school was out for the weekend, and he suffered some 'banter' on the way down the corridor away from the classroom.

Bradshaw cleaned his board, wiping away the mass of equations he'd set to the consternation of his year 9 class. It had been a tough lesson – he should have known better to introduce unknowns on both sides of an equation on a Friday afternoon – but they were a good bunch really. Not a single one of them liked maths, but they seemed to like him, which was half the battle. His old mentor, a long time ago, had always said *'you're not here to be liked, but it sure helps if you are'.*

His desk was its usual mess: stacks of memos marked urgent, even though they weren't; pots of pens, some for students, some for him, most not working; a tray full of calculators with missing lids and coloured in buttons, and, to top it all, two stacks of exercise books. He cursed his bad planning – why take in two sets of books on a Friday? *Rookie mistake.* With a heavy sigh, he put the first pile on a desk at the front of the room. Purple pen in hand – whatever was wrong with red? – he started marking. Almost immediately, he stopped and wheeled himself back to his computer.

Thirty seconds later, Spotify kicked in and Porcupine Tree's latest blasted out of speakers more used to maths explanation videos performed with an Irish accent. Oliver grinned as the music began to soothe away the worst of the day. The marking caught his eye, and he groaned. *Better get on with it.*

Half an hour later, he was halfway through the set. He'd been encouraged to use codes to help address what the students didn't understand, and it sped things up, halving the time it took to mark the books. *Maybe I'll get a weekend after all.* He had a PowerPoint with four different key areas highlighted, each labelled A, B, C or D and was now speeding through the books, writing a letter for each student. Not one said what he was really thinking: *Did you listen to a single word I said?*

"Hey Oliver."

He turned around in his chair, giving the impression of being startled. Bailey Cook grinned at him. Bailey, a PE teacher, was still in good enough shape to be admired by most of the female students, and quite a few of the boys leant in his doorway.

"Pub mate," Bailey said. "You haven't forgotten, have you?"

"Just finishing a set before I head out," Oliver said. He hadn't forgotten but was hoping to slip away unnoticed. Socialising wasn't a strong point of his – what if he made a mistake? Let something slip? Revealed a little too much of his past?

"No worries, boss." It didn't matter what role you had in school, you were 'boss' to Bailey. "How much longer do you want?"

"Half hour?"

"No problem. See you in the car park?"

"Yep. Thanks, mate."

Bailey left him to it and Oliver kept marking, trying to hide his disappointment.

2

Oliver finished early and packed up the other set of books into his rucksack. He made his way downstairs, heading out of the building. It was only 4:30, but the place was already deserted. Even the head-teacher had gone, which was unusual. He fished his mobile out and texted his wife.

Didn't get away with it. See you later x.

His phone buzzed as soon as he'd put it back in his pocket.

You might have fun. Try it!

And then, almost as an afterthought, *xx.*

He grinned and put the phone away. Her optimism that he would finally relax and make friends, was unfounded, but it made her happy he was trying. Bailey was waiting for him out on the school steps and waved.

"That your missus?"

Oliver nodded.

"Got your pass?"

He gritted his teeth, hoping to hide his irritation. He never needed a 'pass' and hated the phrase anyway. If you married someone that controlling, then one of you had a problem. Bailey was a single man, which was obvious within ten seconds of seeing him with any new female member of staff. He was a one-man-walking-denial of *Me Too*.

"Let's go then."

Bailey unlocked his car with a click of the fob, and they clambered in. Oliver put his backpack in the rear seat.

"You can leave that there till the morning mate, I'll drop it round for you."

"Sure?"

"Of course, it's no bother." Every now and again, the influence of living in Scotland showed in Bailey's accent. Pure South London most of the time, yet the 'no' came out as 'nae'.

He gunned the engine and drove towards the town, much too fast.

3

The evening was getting messy, despite Oliver's best efforts at keeping the pace of alcohol down. They'd met in The World's End, joining half of the school's staff at the bar. A couple of hours later, and Oliver was regretting not eating as pint number five was placed in front of him. *Going to pay for this tomorrow.* Sense had long since caught the last bus home and he took a grateful sip. There were ways he could avoid a hangover, but he didn't want to explore them.

Most of the staff had already gone home, many of them driving, some after a little more alcohol than they should, and just the die-hards remained. Bailey was in the corner with the new young English teacher, regaling her with tales of how he was named after a character in *It's A Wonderful Life*. She was looking confused, which only served to highlight how young she looked.

Talking to young people about classic films always made him feel old. Bailey hadn't clocked he was on to a loser, which made the remaining staff laugh. They discussed plans for the weekend, which varied from sleeping and marking, to hiking and paddleboarding. Oliver said he was spending time with his family, and thankfully no-one pushed him too hard on that.

What would he say anyway? *We stay at home, avoiding anyone who may recognise us. We don't really have friends, so we just stick to the three of us. No, we don't have a dog. Used to. It didn't end well.*

Oliver shuddered. He needed to stop drinking. If his wife hadn't suggested it, he wouldn't have come. She said they could relax now – no-one was looking for him up here. They'd stopped years ago.

"Need a piss," he muttered, standing on unsteady legs. A couple of the teachers laughed at his state, but not in a mean way. They were happy he was there, telling him he should join them more often. Oliver staggered to the toilet, not needing any signs or directions as he could smell it.

He opened the door to the toilet and gagged. Puddles of piss sat under each urinal and the stench emanating from the solitary cubicle meant he didn't want to go near there. Underlying those overpowering smells lay something else.

Something he hadn't smelt for a while.

Something that meant trouble.

4

Two blokes stood in the toilet, one leaning on the cubicle, the other finishing up washing his hands – or at least pretending to. They both stared at him as he opened the door. Oliver recovered from his shock at the animalistic smell coming from them and staggered into the doorway, bouncing against the frame.

"Soz," he pretended to hiccup, slurring his words, "thought this was the way out." He turned to leave but found his way barred by a third man who appeared behind him. *How the hell didn't I see him? Smell him?* The answer to that question was easy: alcohol and complacency dulled his senses. The man's bulk filled the corridor and Oliver had no choice but to take a step back into the toilet. The large man followed him, easing the door closed behind him.

"Wassah going on?" Oliver cursed his drinking. First time he'd let himself go for nearly a decade and here they were, finally. His kind.

"Cut the act, we're not here to hurt you." The smallest of the men, dressed bizarrely in clothes at least two sizes too big for him. He looked ridiculous, and his earnest expression hung on him like a cloak. It stood in stark contrast to the menace pouring off the other – bigger, *much* bigger – men.

"I's," another fake hiccup, "jus' out with me pals."

"We know who you are," the man said. "More importantly we know what you are."

Oliver looked between all three, manoeuvring to the urinals by pretending to stagger. The smallest one was in charge, or at least he seemed to think he was. He looked capable, despite the baggy clothes. The biggest one stood in the doorway to the rest of the pub, actually cracking his knuckles like he was a heavy from an eighties' action film. The other one, though, he demanded and commanded Oliver's attention. Almost as big as the guy in the doorway, but something about him oozed danger. Clear blue, intelligent eyes constantly moved, checking out every inch of Oliver. A face which bore the scars of many, many fights.

He was the one to watch.

"I's a bit pished," Oliver said, but he knew he wasn't fooling anyone. How could he get out, back to the others? If he did that, would it put them in danger? Hell, how much danger was *he* in?

The badly dressed man held up a hand, palm out. "Cut the act, okay? I already said we're not here to hurt you."

Oliver straightened, and forced himself to smile, despite the churning in his stomach. "What do you want?"

"My name is Harry, that's Rich, Chris." Nods at the other two, identifying Rich as the dangerous one. Chris and Rich looked broadly similar, so Oliver guessed they were brothers. Why hadn't they ganged up on Harry? Maybe that was coming. Maybe he had no idea how dangerous his companions were.

"We've been on the run for so long I can't remember what it's like to have the same roof over my head for more than a week."

Oliver shrugged; his message clear: *So what?*

"Do you know what it's like out there?" Harry waved an arm, meaning everywhere other than in this toilet. Oliver shook his head. "Last couple of nights, we've been staying in that house up on the hill. You know the one? Only got half a roof, and one of the walls is a pile of stone. Toilet doesn't work and there's nothing to wash with. We had to go to a sports centre today just to shower. You know what that's like?"

Oliver did, but he wasn't going to tell them that. He knew all too well what it was like.

"We, all of us, our kind, are being hunted like vermin. We're being executed in the streets, or in our beds. No trials, no court, no pleas. Nothing. They are exterminating us."

"Who are?"

"Them. The Government. They send their army after us. Sometimes we get away, sometimes we don't." Harry's voice hitched at this last. Tears dotted his red-rimmed eyes and he wiped them away with his palm. "They're not going to stop until we're all in body bags."

"If you're who we think you are," Rich said. "Then you can stop all this."

"Who do you think I am?" Oliver shrugged again. "I'm just a teacher, out on the piss with my colleagues."

Rich snorted and Chris laughed. Harry ran a hand through his hair with a scowl.

"Gary told us all about you. How you healed him. How you can change at will and have decided not to."

"Look, you definitely have the wrong bloke. I don't know anyone called Gary."

"He said he had cancer, but you bit him."

Oliver shook his head. He *could* stop this, right now. All he had to do was—

Yes, let me at them.

He hadn't heard that voice in a while. *Oh, I'm still here. I'm* always *here.*

Something must have changed in his face because Harry took a step back, hitting the sink behind him. He recovered quickly, standing tall again. Neither Chris nor Rich so much as flinched,

"Look," Harry said, "you can help us. We just need them to stop chasing us. We just want them to leave us alone to carry on with our lives. We're not hurting anyone."

Oliver glanced at Rich. *Yes, yes, he's definitely hurt someone. Watch him.* He tried to ignore the voice, but it was getting stronger – something it hadn't done for years. The slightest crack, and there it was.

Fight or flight, that's me. A chuckle inside. *Well, you're flight, I'm all about the FIGHT.*

"Sorry, you want me to do what exactly? Attack the military? Is that it?"

"Well, yeah. You wouldn't be alone though. You'd have us, and anyone else we can find."

"You're nuts."

Harry stepped forward and grabbed Oliver's arm. Oliver shook him off, pushing him in the chest so he staggered backwards. Chris straightened in the doorway. Oliver glared at him.

"Don't touch me."

"I didn't want this to end up in a fight," Harry said, a slight whine in his voice. "I can't keep doing this. They killed my wife, I just, I just—"

Tears did roll now. Oliver felt a twang inside. *This man is broken.*

"No-one knows about me. I'm liked here," Oliver said. "Leave me alone."

"We know you have a family." Rich's voice was calm, quiet and yet the threat was unmissable.

Oliver shrugged. "My family are nothing to do with this. What we are."

He pushed past Chris who didn't try to stop him.

"Please."

The word made him stop, his hand on the toilet door. Oliver glanced back at Harry.

"Please, Mr Stadler," Harry said. "Jack. We need your help."

Oliver narrowed his eyes. "Ain't no-one here with that name. I heard he died a long time ago."

He yanked the door open, almost pulling it off its hinges, and stalked out into the pub. The door thudded closed behind him.

5

Katie Stadler put Josh's clothes away, taking care not to slam any of his bedroom furniture drawers. He was reading to her, getting excited at the adventures of Percy Jackson and his friends. Katie had found the lot bundled together in a charity shop for a little over two pounds a few weeks ago and Josh was already onto the fifth book. He devoured books at a rate she was simultaneously delighted with and envious of. If only she had the time to read like that.

Every now and then he stumbled over a word and she gently corrected him, but in all his reading was excellent. Motherly pride bloomed inside her, but she knew he would probably stop reading by the time his teenage hormones kicked in. *So many kids do, boys especially.*

Finally, she put the last t-shirt away, and sat on the floor next to his bed, giving him her undivided attention. These quiet moments were her favourite in the day: just the two of them, lost in a world of Greek Gods and teenage heroes. She missed it whenever it was Jack's turn to listen.

His alarm clock caught her eye. "Better make this the last paragraph, sweetie, it's getting late."

A look of disappointment creased his face. "But it's the weekend."

"I know, but it's nearly nine o'clock. We can read more tomorrow."

He sighed, but carried on reading, finishing the paragraph like a pro. She lingered in the doorway, hand hovering over the light switch as he put the book away and snuggled down in the bed.

"Hey mum, what's brown and sticky?"

She smiled, and even though she knew the answer said, "I don't know."

"A stick."

"Good one, honey."

"What do you call a man with a car on his head?"

Jack. Oh, how I'd love to hear you call him by that name. "Enough. Lights out."

"Ah c'mon." A Scottish twang to the words there, something which always caught her off guard.

"Make it quick." She smiled at him, indulging his nightly joke fest.

"Jack!" His laughter was genuine and infectious. Her smile became a grin. "Your turn Mum!"

"What do you call a woman sitting on top of a house?"

He frowned.

"Ruth." She pronounced it *roof*.

His frown deepened, then his whole face lightened as he smiled. "That's a good one. Roof. Haha." If there was a better feeling in the world than seeing your child happy, then Katie didn't know what it was.

"Goodnight, Josh."

"Night mum."

She turned off his light and closed the door softly. *Time for wine.*

6

Shit. Shit. Shit.

Jack paused before re-entering the bar. *One night. One fucking night out with some friends.* He'd let his guard down and now this? He thought about returning to the toilet and ripping the three men apart. Deep inside, but not as deep as an hour ago, the Wolf laughed. This was why he'd been so careful, for *years*.

"I'm in charge," he muttered to himself, taking a deep breath and reciting Fibonacci numbers to get himself calm. *Sure you are, Jack.* He gritted his teeth at the voice, getting to 987 in the sequence before he felt in control.

He knew what he had to do.

Yes, go back in there and rip them apart.

No. That wasn't the answer. Violence didn't solve anything.

He had to get home. To Katie and Josh.

7

Bailey was onto a winner here. The new English teacher was well fit, laughed at his jokes and seemed to be into him. Sure, the night had started rocky, with his explanation of *It's A Wonderful Life* falling flat. Maybe she'd have found it funnier if he'd been called Clarence. Maybe she was too young.

Maybe he was too old.

Nah.

He swigged some more beer down, wondering how long she'd be in the toilet. Her absence gave him a chance to fish around for her name. He knew the surname was Fisher, but what the hell was her first name? It said T on her staff badge, which, for some inexplicable reason, she was still wearing. Tina? Something like that.

A loud noise from the other side of the bar made him look up. Everyone turned at the bang, and then Oliver walked into the bar. If he was embarrassed at everyone staring at him, he didn't say anything. Actually, he looked furious. Really, properly, angry. *What the hell?*

Oliver stalked over to the table. He put his hands flat on the sticky table and stared at Bailey like he was trying to remember who he was. The room had been fuzzy until a moment ago and came back into focus as he stared at Oliver.

"You alright mate?"

"I need your car."

"Fuck's sake mate, neither of us can drive."

"I need it now, *mate.*"

Bailey held up both hands, the universal sign for *calm down*. Judging by the expression on Oliver's face, it didn't work. "Seriously, Oliver, we're battered. Let's have another pint and get a cab, yeah?"

"Give me your fucking keys Bailey." Oliver gritted his teeth, and something flashed in his eyes.

Bailey swallowed hard, feeling his bladder loosen, but thankfully not let go. *Not a good look to piss yourself in front of a potential shag.* "Sure, sure thing, mate." He rummaged in his pocket and pulled out the keys. "You sure?"

Oliver snatched the keys from his hand and left without another word.

Bailey reached for his pint, relief flooding through him. His hand shook, but thankfully the glass wasn't full. He drained it and put the glass back on the table.

"Another?" Tina or whatever asked from the bar. He nodded, giving a smile that didn't feel like his best. At least his hand shook less when he returned his glass to the table.

Maybe another pint would make him forget Oliver's eyes changing colour.

Maybe another pint would make him forget his *teeth* getting longer.

Somehow, he doubted it.

CHAPTER 5

1

The Wolf made it easy to sober up – something he'd never really understood, but for which he was grateful now. Jack gripped the wheel hard and drove far too fast down roads not designed for those speeds. Nothing came the other direction, something else to be thankful for.

Home had never seemed so far away.

As he drove, he had time to think. Time to reflect on who those men were. How had they known who he was? How had they been able to find him? No-one knew where he was – not even Knowles.

Had it been Clarkey? Was that it? Clarkey had been the only person who figured it out, but surely he wouldn't have told anyone? Clarkey had terminal cancer, but he'd been so warm, so welcoming and friendly when the Stadlers arrived in Losthorn. Clarkey had helped bring Josh out of his shell – the one created by too many moves, too many midnight flits.

Katie had persuaded Jack to help him, knowing they'd have to send him away. Something about Originals together wasn't right: they fought uncontrollably. But she'd wanted him repaid for his kindness and so Jack had bitten him. They explained why he'd have to leave and also why telling anyone about what had happened would put Jack in danger. He wouldn't have talked.

Would he?

Jack thumped the steering wheel. All this time in Scotland. All this time settled and actually carving out a life. Even returning to teaching had felt like the past was truly behind them; that the future was bright.

And now, now the wolves had found him again. They always wanted something, and that usually left innocent people dead. When they'd left Huntleigh, he'd sworn that was it and he'd never kill again. He'd stay hidden, leave the Wolf buried in Devon.

It had worked.

For ten years, it had worked.

2

Harry stood in the car park, watching the taillights fade from view. Next to him, Rich continued to work on perfecting his scowl.

"That could have gone better."

Harry turned to him. "Why did you bring up his family? What did you think was going to happen? He thought you were threatening him."

"I was."

Chris sniggered. *Always bloody sniggering.*

"Why? You know he could rip us apart, right?"

Again with the snigger. Harry's head pulsed again, sharp pain firing across his brow. He clenched his jaw, feeling his teeth grind. A vein in his forehead throbbed.

"I'd like to see him try." Rich's scowl threatened to swallow his face.

Typical macho bullshit. "Mate, he's an Original."

Rich laughed at that. "They're a fucking myth, *mate*, you smoking the same shit as your wife?"

If Chris sniggered again, Harry would have to rip his throat out. He saw Chris clutching his neck as blood poured between his fingers. Blood bubbles formed and burst as he bled out. Even as fresh pain took flight across his head, he gave a humourless grin. *Yeah, that would be satisfying.*

"Originals are real. Or they were." Harry hated the whine in his voice.

"Just like Robin Hood, or, I don't know, fucking Jesus or something," Rich said, squaring his shoulders and stepping a little closer to Harry.

"Fucking Jesus. That's gross, dude," Chris said.

Rich and Harry stared at him, both wearing identical *what-the-fuck?* expressions. Chris grinned, realising he'd said something stupid. *He's a fucking idiot.*

"Originals. He's no Original." Rich spat a large glob of phlegm into a plant pot. "That's like saying a priest is God on Earth or something. It's just stupid."

"Gary said he healed him."

"Yeah, but *Gary* was off his tits on dope and crack." Rich said, rolling his eyes like a teenager in detention.

"What if he was telling the truth?"

"Then Stadler would have helped us. He'd be so powerful he could rule the world."

Harry thought about that. *Rule the world? Really?* Since he'd been made a wolf, nearly twenty years ago, he'd heard stories of Originals – mostly from people who'd been to Germany. Some bloke had tried to unite all the different wolf clans around ten years ago. What was his name again? Harry couldn't remember, but it all turned out to be bollocks anyway. The clans attacked a military base, trying to free Stadler and had been massacred.

This he did know, first hand. He and Flo barely escaped with their lives. The real shit show had started when some army bloke went AWOL. A service station and then a village in Devon were attacked, complete with CCTV footage showing wolves in action. Soon after that, national outcry led to military action on British soil.

Wolves were now hunted.

They'd gone from anonymity, creatures of stories and myths, to a hunted endangered species in a few short months. The army declared the mission a success several years ago and scaled back their operation. That didn't mean no hunting though, did it?

Just no headlines.

A whole section of the dark web emerged, people trying to band together, trying to help wolves. Most of them were abroad, and the number of British sites dwindled on a daily basis.

Things were getting desperate.

"If he won't help us, then we're screwed." This was the first sensible thing Chris had said. Maybe ever.

Harry couldn't help but agree. "Maybe he'll come round?"

Rich snorted.

"I want to try him again. He has a family. *I* had a family." Harry paused, wishing the pain in his head would go away. *What a time to get a stress migraine.*

"I don't think he'll give much of a shit," Rich said.

"Exactly." Chris was back to sniggering after every one of his brother's words.

"Please, Rich. Let's try again."

Rich nodded. "He has a family."

Something about the way he said those words made Harry's blood run cold.

3

Katie put the glass of wine down and gave up on Netflix. Nothing was holding her attention. Typical that with Jack out, she couldn't find anything that looked even remotely interesting. It was all superheroes, one-word titular detective shows or a fucking reality show. She was in no mood for any of that. Josh was already fast asleep, she knew, as she'd already been and checked on him. Twice.

She sighed, acknowledging at least to herself that she was a little stressed, and not all down to her job. Her work was a lot less taxing than Jack's, just some reception work at a local primary school, but it got her out of the house. One thing she'd struggled with until a few years ago was the change of name. Remembering to call Jack 'Oliver' in public; actually responding anytime anyone called her 'Amelie'. At least she no longer embarrassed herself by blanking people using that name.

She stood and looked out the window. Her reflection stared back: a few more lines; a couple of greys breaking out at her temples, but overall, she couldn't complain. It was fully dark outside now, with very few streetlights illuminating anything close by which meant they had a great view of the stars. Sometimes the Aurora Borealis made an appearance, which always felt special. She had to admit it was beautiful up here, but she missed Devon all the same. *Probably time to let that go.*

She knew why she was restless. Jack hadn't been out in so long, she didn't quite know what to do with herself without him. *Pathetic.*

Didn't make it any less true though. When had she become so dependent on him? *Ten years on the run, that's when.*

"Fuck it," she said, and refilled her wine.

Headlights appeared at the top of the road, sweeping across the front of the house and approaching far too quickly. Katie had money on it being that nobhead Bailey, driving whilst 'only a couple' over the limit, and shook her head as the car screeched to a halt by the gate.

When Jack got out of the car, she knew something was very, very wrong.

4

Two mugs of tea, long since cold, sat between them. They held hands over the table, hers far more lined than his, both deep in thought.

"How did they find you?" Katie said at last.

"It can only have been Clarkey. Anything else is too much of a coincidence." He'd run through everything that happened in the pub, and what he thought it meant.

"I knew you shouldn't have helped him." Katie pulled a face. It had, of course, been her idea. Clarkey and Jack had hit it off immediately. They had their shared experience. Both wolves. Both fugitives from the Government. She never really understood how they knew about each other, but Jack explained it came down to *smell*.

Katie and Jack had been living in Losthorn for nearly six years. Clarkey became like a surrogate uncle to Josh, and even knew their real names. He'd not slipped up once and sometimes had seemed to forget they weren't who they said they were. Their expanded circle of friends was down to him.

He'd introduced Jack to the nobhead Bailey, who in turn got Jack some supply work at his school. A term's worth of supply turned into a couple of years and then a permanent contract. If not for Clarkey and Bailey, Jack wouldn't have got that job and they'd have run out of money years ago.

"He was good to us," Jack said.

"Yes, but we shouldn't have let him go."

"We had no choice. I couldn't risk another situation like with Bryant." Jack had no desire to revisit that memory: how he couldn't control himself whenever Bryant was around; how they would both change instantly and attack. Bryant nearly killed Jack, and, as far as most of the world was concerned, *had* killed him, before Katie shot Bryant and he was cut into pieces before he could heal. Knowles had buried his body in the cave Jack had fallen into a lifetime ago and then sealed it with explosives. No-one was getting near those bones without serious excavation equipment.

For the last ten years, Jack had kept the Wolf at bay. *Not even Year 9 last thing on a Friday brings it close to the surface.* He smiled at the thought: what would that do for classroom management? *Hey kids, if you don't start paying attention, I'll turn into a bowel loosening massive wolf and eat you...*

Ten years. Until tonight. Some beers and a chance meeting with a band of wolves had nearly brought the Wolf out. Jack shuddered. *Scary times. The Wolf is not the answer.*

You sure?

"So, what do we do now?"

"They told me where they're staying. I'm going to pay them a visit."

Katie blanched. "And do what?" She studied him, from the thin set of his lips to the anger clear in his eyes. "Actually, scrap that, I don't want to know."

"I'm just going to talk to them," he said. "Honestly, just talk. I'm not *that* guy."

"You already told them to piss off in the pub."

"Yes, but I want to make sure they got the message."

Katie scooped up both mugs and poured them down the sink. Her bottle of wine was still half full, and she reached for it.

"Leave that."

She opened it and poured some into her glass from earlier, made eye contact then poured some more.

Jack sighed. "That was childish."

"Yeah, but you know better than to tell me not to have a drink."

"I'd like you to take Josh and go away. Just for a few days, until this blows over."

She looked at him over the top of her glass as she downed half of it in one go. Even angry, her eyes captivated him. "Go where, Jack? We're not exactly overflowing with friends."

"Go to London for a couple of nights. Get a hotel. Take Josh to see the sights. He'd love it."

"London? Seriously?" She put the glass down, back to him now, with hands on the counter. Her shoulders were tense, and he hugged her from behind. She stiffened, then relaxed into the hug, resting the back of her head on his shoulder.

"I don't know how this will go," he said, voice gentle. Her perfume was intoxicating, even without his Wolf senses. "I don't know how many of them there are."

"You said three?"

"Yeah, three in the pub. But how many in the house? There might be some in other places."

She turned and hugged properly, her arms tight around his waist. "I don't want to be apart from you."

When this had all started, Jack had been pronounced dead. She'd even received a pay-out from his pension for death in service. It took her a long time to forgive him, but given he'd been kidnapped by the British army, she eventually had.

"It'll be a few days," Jack said. "Maybe even just two."

"Two days I can do. It'd be good to show Joshie around the big smoke."

Jack smiled, relaxing as she was coming round to his idea.

"Take lots of photos," he said. "Come on, I'll help you pack."

"Now?" She pulled away. "You want me to go *now*?"

He nodded. "There's a train from Inverness just before five. Slow train, will get you to London in the afternoon."

"Why—"

"What if they come here Katie? They found me in the pub, and I don't think it was by accident. They could come here, and I don't want you – and definitely not Josh – here if that happens."

"I can take care of myself."

He sighed. "I know that, honey. Believe me I know." She'd been the one to kill Bryant after all. "But what about Josh? What if he sees me change?" Jack felt sick at the thought. Somehow, he didn't think his son would think it was cool his dad could change into a huge Wolf and rip people apart without breaking sweat.

Katie drank the rest of the wine, moving away from him. "Christ, Jack."

"We knew this might happen."

"Yeah, but the constant panic they'd find us has kind of faded over the last few years, you know what I mean?"

He did. At first, when they'd not stayed anywhere longer than three months, they'd not even bothered to unpack. The thought of more wolf packs finding them and then carnage like in Huntleigh was more terrifying than the wolves themselves. Losthorn was remote and, even though tourists came in the summer, it was never that busy. It had been easy to relax here – and it began to feel like home.

"Look, I'll speak to them. Get rid of them. Convince them to leave us alone."

"And if you can't?"

He didn't say anything but couldn't look her in the eye either. She nodded, and stomped up the stairs, heading to pack.

I'm not that guy anymore.

You sure, Jack?

5

Josh wasn't happy at being woken, even for a surprise. He yawned, with all his limbs extended, his whole body stretched and twisted in his bed. *Christ, if I did that, I'd put my back out.*

"It's too early," he said as soon as he looked at the clock.

"Yeah, but we've got to get to the train," Katie said, putting a couple of folded t-shirts into a bag. She threw his favourite Star Wars one at him. "Put this on," she said.

"Chewie, yes!" He grinned at her and shrugged his pyjamas off. T-shirt on, he pulled pants and jogging bottoms on, then a jumper. "Where we going?"

Katie cricked her neck, feeling the tension there and hoping it didn't show. He wasn't that surprised at being woken in the middle of the night – maybe he remembered those midnight journeys from places all those years ago.

"It's a surprise," she said.

"Tell me!" His bottom lip was out, making him look more like a four-year-old.

She went to the bathroom, returning with his toothbrush (a stormtrooper handle) and shower-gel. "If I tell you, it won't be a surprise, will it?"

"I don't like surprises," he said.

No, I don't suppose you do. "Okay, but are you sure you want to know?"

"Yes, yes, yes! A million times yes."

She couldn't help smiling at him. What was it about the innocence of youth? A little of the tension in her shoulders eased. "Okay, I thought we could go to London for a few days. An early birthday present."

"My birthday was last month."

"I meant a late present."

"Why didn't I get to open this then?"

Questions, questions, questions. All the bloody questions. She forced herself to stay calm – not easy given the circumstances. "We weren't sure it would happen," she said eventually. "Dad couldn't get the time off, but he said to go anyway."

"Dad's not coming?"

"No, he has to work, sweetheart." *No, he's about to face down a pack of wolves and maybe tear them into small pieces.*

"So do you."

"I have a few days owed to me." Did she really have to explain everything to him? "We're going on an adventure. Just me and you. It'll be fun."

"Be more fun with Dad," he said.

Brutal honesty.

He caught her expression and his face fell. "Sorry Mum, I didn't mean it wouldn't be fun with you. Just more fun if it was the three of us."

"Good save kid."

She handed him his backpack. "Come on, or we'll miss the train."

6

They stashed their clothes in bags and hid them in the car park. Even though the clothes didn't fit him, Harry didn't want to lose them – they were all he had after all. Soon they were running across dark fields on all fours, wind ruffling the fur on their backs. Harry loved this, the feel of the ground pounding beneath his paws, how he could see so clearly despite it being pitch black and the smells – oh the smells!

All wolves had a good sense of smell, even in human form, but as a wolf it was insane. He knew there were cattle up on the hill around half a mile to his right and deer in the woods ahead. He salivated at the thought but forced himself onwards. By the slowing of their step, he knew Chris and Rich had caught scent of the prey too, but they all continued onwards.

A normal wolf could maintain a speed of around thirty miles per hour over short distances – just a couple of miles. The combination of human and wolf however, meant that could be extended for hours. Harry thought he could outrun the other two – whilst they were big, he was faster, smaller, lighter.

He led the way, circling around to a hillock to the north of Stadler's house, keeping the wind in his face. Now was not the time to let Stadler know they were here. Harry sat in shadows of the trees just a few hundred yards from the house and turned back to human.

This was a perfect spot to observe the house. He watched as a pretty woman, maybe early forties but wearing it well, led a boy of around ten to the car, and then Stadler followed them.

Harry looked at Rich, who was still in wolf form. The wolf inclined its head, yellow eyes glowing in the dark.

The Stadlers were fleeing.

7

Inverness wasn't far and as traffic was non-existent given how early in the morning it was, they made good time. Jack kept looking in the rear-view all the same, stiffening any time he saw headlights there. Katie had her hand on his knee, squeezing every time she sensed him tense.

"You said they looked rough. Clothes didn't fit, that kind of thing. Why would they have a car?"

Jack didn't respond, but checking the road ahead and all the mirrors, nevertheless. Katie didn't need to know a pack of wolves could easily run across country and cut them off. He drove as fast as he dared and each time the needle crept past sixty, Katie squeezed his leg again.

He eased off, the anxiety in the pit of his stomach threatening to overwhelm him. The Wolf wanted out, but that would be ridiculous. *Not in front of Josh.* Inverness came into view and he sped to the station, pulling into the small car park out front.

Katie led Josh to the platform whilst Jack bought the tickets. He followed them onto the concourse where they waited by the barriers. Katie hugged him, and kissed him firmly on the lips, earning a 'ewww' from Josh.

Jack grinned and knelt to hug his son. "Look after Mum, okay?"

"I will. I wish you were coming too."

"Me too kiddo." Jack hugged him again. Would this be the last time he saw him? "It's only for a few days. You'll be home before you know it. I want to hear all about it, okay?"

"Can't you come?" Josh was nothing if not persistent. Jack pulled out his phone and tapped an app. Immediately the screen showed a map of the area, with a picture of Josh in a circle just above Inverness station. He showed his son the screen.

"I'll know exactly where you are, all the time," Jack said. "And you can ring me anytime."

"What if you're in class?"

"I'll answer anyway. You're more important than a bunch of students."

Josh nodded, expression solemn. He rattled off Jack's mobile number. "I'll call you when we get there."

Jack ruffled his hair, and Josh pulled away. *Too big for that now.* "Thanks, Squiggs." The use of the nickname made Josh smile. None of them knew where it came from, or who had started it, but it never failed to make Josh happy.

"Be safe," Katie whispered. "Don't do anything stupid."

"I won't. It's just a conversation, I promise."

Katie's expression said she didn't believe him, but he didn't want to drag that up again.

"See you in a couple of days," he said.

She nodded, hugged him again, then took Josh's hand and went through the barrier without a backward look.

Chapter 6

1

The house emerged from the gloom as if a shadow made solid. It stood in its own plot around a hundred metres from the road. A small drystone wall surrounded it, although its days of keeping anything out, or being considered a wall, were long behind it. Several sections were little more than rubble, and grass and weeds threatened to overwhelm it. The enclosed garden didn't look much better. An overgrown lane ran up to the house, where a weathered metal gate somehow still stood.

Jack parked up in a layby. He checked his watch. Still an hour until dawn but he could see as clearly as if it were daylight. The Wolf bubbled dangerously close to the surface. He got out of the car, closing the door with a soft click. In the stillness before dawn, it sounded like a gunshot.

He walked towards the house, knowing there was little point in disguising his approach. They'd be able to smell long before he saw them. His legs felt heavy, with a knot of tension in his back so tight he hunched over to try and ease it.

Closer now and still nothing moved. He couldn't smell anything either, but the debacle in the pub earlier meant he was out of practice with that particular skill. Could you even get out of practice with *smelling*? In different circumstances, he would laugh at himself for how ridiculous he was being.

Less than a hundred yards to go, so they must know he was there by now. Surely?

Birds flew from the trees to his rights in a flurry of squawks and wing beats. He jumped, heart beating a little faster. *This is a bad idea.*

The house loomed over him, dark and oppressive. Jack clambered over the collapsed wall, the smell of damp, rotten wood and fox shit assailing him. *Guess my sense of smell is working.* A battered door with peeling paint barred the way to the rest of the house. There were no wolves here, of that he was certain, so where were they?

Heart now firmly on the verge of overload, he pushed the door open and entered the dark room. The door swung shut behind him, banging in the frame and shaking dust from the ceiling.

The room was dank and dingy. Remnants of a fire sat in the middle of a floor that was more earth than concrete. Plants sprouted around the perimeter, and piles of rubbish dotted the room. Cans of strong lager peppered the rubbish, all looking new and shiny, out of place against the older remains. They may have been here for only a few days, but they'd clearly drunk a lot.

I'd have too, if this is what I had to sleep in.

He shivered, hairs on his arms rising. Something was wrong – more than the state of the room. Someone was coming.

Two things hit him at once.

A scent, out of place: aftershave, just a tang of it, like someone had washed it off, but in a hurry so some remained. The second thing was more shocking; more alarming. He *recognised* the smell.

Jack spun to face the door as it opened slowly. Hinges creaked like a cliche. Jack's eyes scanned the familiar face and then dropped to the thing he carried. A handgun. Held loosely in one hand, like it wasn't anything important. Nothing to see here. He looked at Jack with a grim smile. The handgun shifted in his grip, still not exactly aiming at Jack, but not exactly *not* aiming at him either.

"Hi Jack," Bailey said.

2

"Who?" Jack said.

Bailey shook his head, grin still in place. "Nice try. Come on, mate, I know who you are. I've always known."

"I don't know—"

"Give it up. I know who – and more importantly, *what* – you are."

It felt as if he'd been punched in the gut. He could barely breath, and if he'd thought his heart was going too fast earlier, it had clearly found another gear. *Bailey? How?*

"I need to go," Jack said, but Bailey held a hand up.

"Wherever you're going, I'm coming too."

"The fuck you are."

Bailey shifted his weight, and Jack realised they were almost toe-to-toe. He was also aware of just how big his friend – or supposed friend – actually was. He cursed himself: how could he have been so stupid? How could he have not suspected Bailey had ulterior motives? His willingness to make friends with Jack, despite Jack never going for a drink with him (well, until tonight, and what a mistake that had been), his support for Jack with his teaching, his constant chats at work.

Stupid. Stupid. Stupid.

"Were you ever my friend? Are you working for them?"

"Them?" Bailey frowned. "Who? Who are you talking about? The captain told me to look out for you, so here I am."

"You're not with those blokes from the pub?"

"What blokes?" Bailey took a step backwards, as if realising he was being intimidating. He remained close enough for Jack to smell the stale alcohol on his breath and see the sweat beading on his brow. "Hey, I like you, Jack. This has been the best assignment the captain ever gave me. Kick back in Scotland, teaching kids football and rugby, weekends drinking and shagging? Quality." A rueful grin. "Until tonight."

"Tonight. You set me up."

"Jack, I wanted you out for a beer, mate, that's it. I've no clue what you're talking about."

Jack blinked. *Was he telling the truth?* He tuned in to the Wolf for a moment, listening and smelling. Bailey's heart rate was normal. The sweat on his head could be attributed to alcohol. Nothing out of the ordinary. Except for the gun and his presence in the strange house just before dawn.

"Look, I was cracking on to that new English bird, Tina—"

"That's not her name."

"Whatever, you came over ranting about me keys."

"I needed to get home."

"Your eyes changed, Oliver." Bailey tutted and rolled his eyes. "Jack. I knew something was up. Look, I'm just some annoying twat teaching PE to you, but I'm not stupid." He grinned, acknowledging how much of an understatement the first part was. "I had a few coffees, stopped drinking and borrowed a mate's car. Got to your house, saw it was empty. I thought you might have headed south, train station or just drive all the way. You passed me and of course, I recognised the car."

Jack nodded. He wasn't sure if he could trust Bailey, not yet anyway, but his story sort of made sense. It would've been several hours since a drink, so whilst still over the limit, he would be able to drive without totalling a car.

"So you want to tell me what's going on?"

"Not really," Jack said. "I thought I'd meet some people here."

"People? Like, like *you* people, or just people?"

"No-one's like me," Jack said softly. "Not anymore."

Bailey frowned at that, then fished a phone out of his pocket and clicked on the address book. It looked nothing like the shiny new models he always waved around the staffroom.

"What are you doing?"

"The captain set up protocols for this. If you contacted wolves, or vice versa." He frowned at the screen. "Missed call. Fuck." Bailey rolled his eyes. "Man, this phone has been by my side for years, never rung. Not once." He waved the phone at Jack. "I really thought it was all bullshit until tonight, when your eyes changed. That was pretty fucking freaky, I can tell you. Just about pissed my pants." Bailey grinned.

Yeah, it's all fun and games until the screaming starts. "Hang on, who's this captain? What're you talking about?" Jack knew though, like when you know who's ringing your phone before you even pick it up.

"Mate, I left the military about four years ago. My last CO asked me if I'd come up here and keep an eye on you for a wee boost to my pension. Pretty easy decision really."

"Your CO?"

"Captain Peter Knowles."

3

Of course.

"He knows where I am?"

Bailey shrugged by way of an answer.

"Why didn't you say anything?"

Another shrug. "He told me not to. Said he felt better knowing there was a pair of eyes on you."

Jack snorted. "Did he tell you about me?" A nod. "And?"

Bailey's silence spoke volumes.

"Not such an easy gig after all."

"Yeah." Bailey looked around the room, taking in the rubbish and state of disrepair. "You could've tidied, what with guests coming and all."

"That meant to be funny?"

"Well, yeah, actually, it was."

Jack stared at him as he wandered the room, kicking at random piles of rubbish. *Working for Knowles. All this time.*

"Look, whatever happened tonight wasn't down to me. I wanted a few beers with my mates and to have a crack at the new bird. That's it." Bailey picked something off the floor, examined it, sniffed it, blanched and threw it away. "I have no clue what's going on, apart from you might actually be magic and one of these wolf things we've been trying to get rid of."

Jack sighed and ran a hand through his hair. "How much did Knowles tell you?"

"Not that much, really. Said you were a good wolf, like that was a thing. Told me to call him if anyone I didn't like the look of came to you."

"Didn't like the look of?" Jack smirked.

"Yeah, he's clearly never stood in front of Year Nine."

Despite everything, Jack laughed, and Bailey joined him. It felt good to laugh. "Knowles always thought I was okay for a wolf. What does that even mean? 'Okay for a wolf'. I'm not sure if that makes him a bigoted twat or not."

"The Captain is many things, Jack, but he's not a bigot or racist or any of those things. He's a good guy, really. Not that I'd say that to his face."

"Last time I saw him, he was a sergeant."

"I haven't seen him for a couple of years." He paused, tapping the old phone. "Guess I should speak to him."

"And say what? Three guys approached me in a pub, but now they're gone."

"I went to your house Jack. Katie and Josh aren't there. You're here. You're worried enough. Where are they?"

"Safe."

"Okay, so why have you moved them from your house?"

He's got me there. "The men threatened me. Said they knew I had a family."

"What did they want?"

Can you trust this man? Even as the thought formed, Jack knew the answer. Knowles *was* decent. If he'd sent Bailey, then it would have been with good intentions. *Hopefully.* He took a breath, took the plunge. "They wanted me to help them. Wanted me to join the fight."

Bailey's hand shifted on his handgun, almost imperceptible, but there.

"I told them no," Jack said. "Bailey, put the fucking gun away – I am not a threat to you."

"Yeah, yeah, yeah, sorry." He held up his hand and tucked the gun into a shoulder holster under his jacket. "Been years since I held one of those anyway."

"After I said no, that's when the mean looking one, Rich his name was, mentioned my family. Looks like they've cleared out though, so drama over."

"Hopefully," Bailey said. He didn't sound convinced, but then, neither had Jack. "Where have you put Katie and Josh?"

"No offence, man, but I just found out you've been spying on me for years. Pretty sure you're okay, but I'm not telling you that just yet."

Bailey nodded like not only was he expecting Jack's response, but also respected it. "Fair enough," he said, and then after a long pause, "so what now?"

"I need to go home," Jack said. He sniffed at his armpits and pulled a face. "A shower wouldn't go amiss."

"Fair play. I'll follow you."

Jack inclined his head. "Really?"

"Mate, you're driving my car. Least you can do is get it back to my flat."

4

Jack's head was a mess as he drove. Thoughts collided, each pushing at each other, vying for pole position.

Three men, looking for him to join some crusade. Not dissimilar to what Callum had wanted all those years ago. One important difference: Callum was unhinged – these three just looked desperate.

Katie and Josh, kissing him goodbye.

Bailey, not what he appeared to be. Well, not quite. Clearly, he was a lecherous twat, and he had too much interest in women younger than him, but Knowles trusted him, so that had to be worth something.

Katie, kissing him hello when Josh was in bed.

Harry's desperate eyes when he asked for Jack's help.

Jack punched the steering wheel a few times, frustration bubbling up. *What the hell am I supposed to do?* Harry was right – Jack could make a big difference in the fight against the military. Knowles knew that. Was Bailey here to kill him if it looked like he would flip? Jack didn't think so, but he had to, at least, consider the possibility.

Bailey needed careful watching and handling.

Where had the men gone? Where were they now?

Jack parked the car outside Bailey's flat. It wasn't far to walk back to his own house and maybe the night air would help clear his head, stop it whirling so much. He locked the car and slid the keys onto the wheel as they'd agreed. Jack had deliberately driven back to Bailey's quickly – putting space between them.

He started walking down the road and felt a buzzing in his leg. His mobile. He looked at the screen, then answered it, a smile breaking out on his face as Katie's face came into view. She was holding a glass of wine bigger than her head, a wicked, sexy smile on her face.

His smile did not last long.

CHAPTER 7

1

Alastair Burgess was in his happy place: driving a train across beautiful countryside as the sun came up. He doubted anyone had a better job than him at that moment – maybe Tom Cruise, but he'd be thinking about ways to crash the train for a stunt, and why would anyone want to damage these beautiful beasts? No thank you, Mr Cruise.

He glanced at his watch, which only confirmed he was bang on time. Some drivers didn't give two hoots about timekeeping, but for Alastair it was a source of pride. It also led to his three consecutive employee of the month awards. It would have been four had it not been for COVID.

Alastair unwrapped his sandwich, and bit into it. Pastrami, rocket, bit of cheese and jalapeno peppers. One of the greatest sandwiches known to man. He finished the first, and then saw the rock in the middle of the tracks ahead.

"Shit!"

Alastair was not one for swearing, but it seemed the only appropriate response as he smacked the emergency brakes. The train screeched to a halt, stopping just before the rock.

2

The lights of Inverness faded behind them as the first tendrils of dawn crept over the horizon and snatched darkness from the sky. Josh sat with his face pressed against the window of the train, watching the countryside flash by outside, even though most of it was still shrouded in shadow. He'd sat like that for the forty minutes or so they'd been travelling so far.

"Why don't you get some rest, honey?" Katie said, stroking the back of his head. His hair was so soft – brown like his dad's, but less coarse. His skin was smooth too, the benefits of youth and clean living in Scotland. She could see Jack in him: the curve of his lips, the shape of his nose. His eyes were hers, and though she knew she was biased, she couldn't help thinking what a handsome man he'd grow into.

Just like his dad.

"Not tired," he said, yawning. "Tell me a joke."

She sighed. "I'm not really in a joke telling kind of mood."

His face fell. "Please, Mum?" For a moment, he looked so disappointed her heart nearly shattered.

Well, now I'm the worst mother in the world. Despite their nightly joke off, right then, she couldn't think of any. Apart from a hugely inappropriate one about a priest going fishing. No way she could tell *that* to a ten-year-old.

She went for something tamer. "Why are pirates called pirates?"

He was already laughing. "I don't know. Why?"

"Because they aaarghh." She leaned into to him, closing one eye as she delivered the punchline. *I could listen to him laugh all day.*

"That's awful mum," he said.

"Blame your father."

"He's been telling me that joke since I was three."

A man made his way down the corridor. He wore a pair of jeans and a t-shirt and seemed to be looking at her. A knot of anxiety formed in her stomach. She lay a hand on Josh's leg, trying not to squeeze too hard. He needn't know how she was feeling. To him, this needed to be an adventure.

The man stopped frowning as he checked the seat reservation against a ticket on his phone. He sat, his back to them. She breathed out, trying to release the tension. It failed.

"Mum, what's white and swings through trees?"

More jokes. She smiled at him, but it felt forced even to her. *Can he tell? Does he know how worried I am?*

"Tarzan the fridge."

She laughed despite herself. "Did Daddy tell you that one?"

He nodded.

"Do you get it? Do you even know who Tarzan is?"

"He was raised in the jungle."

Oh, okay then. The door to the carriage opened again, and another man stepped in. He was a big guy, really muscled across his chest and his t-shirt strained with the effort of trying to contain it all. The days were warming up, but a t-shirt only at that time in the morning? The knot became a ball.

"What's white and blue and swings through trees?"

Why hadn't she asked Jack for a description of the men in the pub? All he'd said was big and badly dressed. Did this guy count?

"Tarzan the fridge in a denim jacket."

The man strolled down the centre aisle, eyes straight ahead. Hair shaved apart from on top, where it was brushed forward into a severe straight line. Hoop earring in his right ear. Heavy looking gold chain around his neck. Right arm a sleeve of tattoos, his left bare. He grinned

at her, nodding at Josh, and slid into a seat on the other side of the aisle
to them. Phone in hand as soon as he was settled, he popped in some
white headphones and ignored her.

"Do you get it, mum?"

Katie breathed out, feeling the ball ease a little. *Just someone on the
way home after a night out in Inverness probably. Maybe the walk of
shame.* She laughed at the thought. It had been a long, long time since
she had done a walk like that: heading home, slightly worse for wear,
in your previous night's clothes.

"Sorry, honey, say it again."

The train stopped so abruptly her head rocketed forward and nearly hit the seat in front. The big guy's phone flew out of his hand,
bouncing into the aisle. He tried to grab it as it spun in the air, but
only managed to slap it further down the aisle.

"Fucking thing," he said, then flashed a sheepish smile at Katie and
Josh. *Sorry,* he mouthed.

She smiled back, letting him know it wasn't a problem, then looked
out the window again.

"Why have we stopped, Mum?"

"Trains stop all the time Squiggs." *They do, they always stop at
random points on the line. Nothing to worry about.*

Nothing at all.

3

Alastair hit the tannoy button. "I'm sorry for our abrupt stop, ladies
and gentlemen. There is a small blockage on the tracks. We'll be on
our way soon."

He peered out of the huge windscreen. The rock didn't look that big now he was closer, but it would definitely have derailed the train. Probably. Maybe.

So, option one: call back to Inverness, inform them of the blockage, wait for hours for them to send someone to clear it. Irate passengers wouldn't help anyone, and it would cost him this month's employee award. Option two: get out and deal with it. No-one needed to know, and they'd be on their way in two minutes. An acceptable delay.

Alastair nodded to himself and opened the driver's door. Out of the cabin, he shivered. The tree line on the far side of the tracks looked much darker from out here. He swallowed hard, then laughed at himself. One to tell the boys on their next outing. *Yeah, I moved a rock and got spooked because trees are dark. Who knew?*

He bent over the rock and lifted it. Or at least, he tried to lift it, but it was a lot heavier than it looked. After a couple of attempts, which did nothing except exacerbate his back problem, he gave up.

Maybe there was someone on the train who could help.

Alastair stood, just in time to see something move from the trees.

4

Chris's first bite ripped out the man's throat, severing his vocal cords and windpipe in one go. The man didn't look surprised, more pissed off, but Chris didn't care. He dragged his claws along the man's chest, spilling his delicious internal organs on the ground. Chris went to feast but felt a nudge in his side.

Rich, in wolf form, gestured at the train with his head.

Chris nodded. *This is going to be awesome.*

5

Callum Triggs looked at his watch again. The driver said a couple of minutes, and that had been at least a couple of minutes ago, so what was the delay? Condensation covered the window next to him, and he cleared a patch with his sleeve. The fabric soaked the water up, revealing how dirty the window underneath had been. *Disgusting.*

He peered out into the gloom but couldn't see anything. A bit of movement at the edge of his circle of clarity. *What is that?*

Nothing. Just a lump next to the track, like the announcement said.

So why aren't we moving?

The door to the carriage opened. The front door. The one to the driver's compartment.

Callum frowned and then cried out in shock.

In the doorway stood a large, well-muscled, naked, man.

A couple of seconds later – no more than two heartbeats really – the screaming started.

6

Katie heard a muffled noise, like a shout. *What's that?* More noise from the next carriage. Katie leant into the aisle, a frown creasing her brow. The door to the other carriage was almost entirely glass, surrounded by a metal frame, with rubber seals in the middle. She could see the first few rows in the carriage.

What the hell?

Icy fingers clutched her gut. Someone ran towards their carriage, but they fell, stumbling out of view.

More of that muffled noise.

A young woman appeared on the other side of the carriage door. She had her back to them, focus entirely on something unseen further along the aisle. The door to their carriage opened and the young woman backed in, only turning once the doors hissed shut. She was pale and wide eyed, appearance a sharp contrast to the smart business suit she wore. She staggered forward, clutching a seat to remain upright.

Katie stared at her. Something was wrong.

There. On her suit leg, standing bright against the grey of the material. A red stain, slowly darkening as it soaked into the material.

Blood.

The woman was crying now, ugly tears creasing her face. A low noise was coming from her, and it took Katie a moment to realise she was trying to speak.

"They.... killed.... him...."

"Josh," Katie said. "Up we get, time to go."

The big guy strode towards the woman in the suit. He took her arm and guided her to a seat. She was shaking, her body convulsing as she tried to gulp for air. He was talking to her, but she had a vacant expression on her face Katie recognised only too well.

Shock.

Behind her, the door slid open again, and, this time, Katie, definitely, unequivocally heard a scream.

And a growl.

Her insides went cold. No more anxiety, just outright terror. She knew that noise, even if she hadn't heard it in a while. In a heartbeat, she was back in Huntleigh, trying to get Jack back and keep him safe.

"What's wrong? You're hurting me."

She stared at Josh and realised she was pulling at him, almost dragging him out of the seat. "Sorry sweetheart, but we got to go."

Go? Go where exactly? Off the train. Get off the fucking train.

The door slid open again. A large brown and white wolf crept into the carriage, teeth bared. Saliva drooled from its mouth, and yellow eyes glared with baleful rage at everyone in the carriage.

"Fuck!" The big guy stumbled backwards, away from the woman and more importantly, the wolf. He tripped over his own feet and landed heavily on his backside. He scrambled backwards, but his legs failed to support him as panic took over.

The other man stood and, to his credit, tried to pull the big guy to his feet. They flailed at each other for a moment, until the big guy realised he wasn't being attacked. The wolf hadn't moved, keeping the door open with its considerable bulk.

"What's that?" Josh pointed at the wolf. Katie pushed his hand down and pulled him into the aisle.

"It's a wolf, honey."

"Cool."

Not cool. Horrible. Unnatural. Terrifying.

The wolf moved. It surged forward with a speed that made a mockery of its size. In a heartbeat it covered the distance to the two men and grabbed the big guy's foot. A snarl, a shake of the head and his foot was in the wolf's mouth as it backed away from the man. He screamed as blood pulsed out of the stump.

"Holy shit," Katie said.

The sight galvanised the would-be rescuer. He turned and fled, pushing past Katie and slamming her against the seat in the process. Josh was still in the gap between seats so at least he didn't get hit. She didn't think he'd seen the severing of the foot either.

She hoped.

The woman in the suit hadn't moved. More blood splashed onto her, but she didn't seem to notice. She sat, shaking and crying as the wolf crouched next to her, eating the foot without a care in the world. It started with ripping the jeans, socks and trainer off and was already gnawing at bones. The foot's owner lay prone in the aisle, passed out, which was small mercy for what was inevitable.

The wolf dropped the bone and moved towards him.

Katie pushed Josh further back into the gap between seats. She looked back along the length of the carriage, away from the wolves. The door at the end led to the outside, to the tracks. Out there, they'd be caught and slaughtered in seconds.

Their chances in here were no better.

7

Harry walked along the train, searching passengers faces as he did. He was tired from the cross-country run, but adrenaline kept him going. Katie Stadler was somewhere on this train. Their plan – no Rich's plan – was simple: take Katie and her son, use them as leverage to make Jack see sense. If he wouldn't help directly, then the least Jack could do would be to bite them all, make them more powerful.

In his garbled recollections, Gary hadn't really explained what Jack had done. Bitten him, yes, but had that turned him into an Original? Harry somehow doubted it. Gary hadn't looked too clever back in the flat when the soldiers stormed it. If he'd been an Original, he'd have healed and sorted them all out. Harry knew the stories about Jack being an Original, but did that mean he really could make them more powerful?

Really?

Rich strode ahead of him, naked but still intimidating. Scars criss-crossed his back, reminders of scraps with other wolves. Those fights only ever ended one way: with a dead wolf.

Harry swallowed rising bile as they passed a couple of corpses. Passengers shied away from him, grateful to be alive but terrified of what would come next. Harry felt tiny next to Rich, but even so he was in better shape than most. The pheromones coming from the passengers made him feel better. More powerful.

This isn't you.

Flo's voice, clear in his head but maybe *this* was him now. Maybe it was time to embrace his wolf. Chris and Rich had, a long time ago, and they were completely at ease here. Chris bounded ahead, his brown and white fur streaking through the carriages, heading to the rear of the train. Only one carriage remained, so that must be where the Stadlers were.

He heard screams and jogged to catch up. Rich also ran forward. A man in a cheap suit lay in the middle of the aisle, missing a foot and his throat ripped out. Harry could smell other passengers still in the carriage, all hiding between the seats. *Like that will protect them!* Blood pulsed in his head, heart hammering in his chest. More smells assailed him: piss, shit, blood, fear. He zeroed in on the acrid scent of urine.

A young man, mid-twenties, cowered in the gap, his grey trousers stained dark around the crotch.

I should rip his heart out.

An overwhelming urge to hurt this man overcame him and Harry lurched forward, ready to change. He stopped himself when he saw the fear in the young man's eyes.

This is not *you.* Flo's voice again, but given she was dead, she had no power of him anymore.

No.

He snarled at the man instead, earning a whimper and a cry of terror. Before the wolf could take more of a hold, Harry stalked back down the aisle, hurrying after Rich's retreating back.

Hurrying towards the screams.

8

The wolf sniffed and growled. Katie's legs shook as she reached into her pocket and fished out her mobile phone. Josh watched her with wide eyes.

"I'm scared, Mum."

He whispered the words, but they hit her like he'd screamed them. She pulled him into an uncomfortable hug, which was more like her squeezing his head than an actual hug. She put her fingers to her lips, then unlocked her phone.

Last time she had faced a wolf, she had a machine gun in her hands. The terror of that day had faded over time, but she did still have the occasional nightmare about it.

But now, here she was again, face to face with a creature from legend. Only this time, she had nothing except her fists and a sharp word. Given the last time she'd punched someone had been about thirty years ago (Karen Moorstock, the slag), she only really had her words.

If only Jack was here. She felt more than a little disgusted at herself for the thought. She'd never needed a man to defend her before. Hell, she'd taught herself to shoot a shotgun when Jack was first declared dead.

She pressed the direct dial button for Jack without taking her eyes from the approaching wolf. With a shaking hand, she raised the mobile.

The wolf rose up, fur running back into the body until a large, well-built man stood where it had. He was naked and scratched his balls whilst grinning at her.

"Mrs Stadler, I presume." The man sniffed deeply, the not-really-a-smile never leaving his face. "I can smell the stench of your husband all over you."

Great. A fucking dickhead and a wolf. The whole package.

"Jack," she said, not giving the man the satisfaction of looking where he was scratching. "We're in trouble. We love you very much."

Two other men entered the carriage, both also naked. These other two were smaller, but one only just. The one at the rear was about the same size as Jack and would be handsome in any other circumstances. He frowned, surveying the carriage like a card player hiding a bad hand.

The second biggest had the beady eyes and hard face of a life of difficulties, and she wondered if that were due to being a wolf, or if he had been like that before. Scars crossed his chest, some disappearing around his thick torso. There was a similarity between the two biggest wolves – brothers?

The one at the back pushed forward, past the others. "Mrs Stadler," he said. "You need to come with us."

"Go with him lady!" a man's voice, from behind her. She had no idea there was anyone there and jumped at his voice. She stood, hoping her trembling legs would support her weight.

"Get fucked," she snarled, forcing her anger to mask her terror.

"Mum!"

"Sometimes it's the right word, Squiggs."

The man, who was really a wolf, grinned at her. "I like you, Mrs S, you're a woman after my own heart."

"If only I were single." Her voice dripped with sarcasm.

"Drop the phone, please." This came from the smallest of them. Katie studied him for a moment, thinking he seemed the most reasonable of the three. The one to work on.

"And if I don't?"

"Then Chris here will rip you limb from limb."

She shifted her gaze to the biggest one. He leered at her, suggesting in a look that perhaps, ripping her apart wouldn't be the first thing he'd do. Josh snatched the phone from her hand and threw it at the one in front. He caught it with one hand.

"Leave my mum alone," Josh said. He looked so much like Jack, even sounded like him, she thought her heart would burst with pride.

"Kiddo, let the grown-ups talk, okay?" The one with the phone looked at it, then raised it. "Hi Jack, in the coming days, just remember this is your fault."

9

"If you harm her, I will kill you all."

Jack was breathing hard, his limbs on fire. The Wolf strained at its leash, wanting out. Wanting these men who were threatening its pack.

"Empty threats, Jack. Where are you? Back at home? Or up at our house?"

"I will find you."

"We're counting on it."

He could hear the smile in Rich's voice.

"What do you want?"

"We told you. We want your help."

"Kidnapping my wife and kid is not the way to go about it."

"That's what Harry said," Rich said with a sniff. "He's a pussy too."

"Stay there, I'll come to you."

"Oh that's good Jack; There's a good boy."

Rich emphasised the *good*, like he was talking to a puppy. Dark spots appeared at the edges of Jack's vision, threatening to overwhelm him. Jack took several deep breaths, forcing himself to calm. If the Wolf came now, this would end in a blood bath.

"I'm warning you—"

"No, Jack, you have no cards to play here." A rustling, a scrape of stubble on the microphone. Jack heard Rich asking about a camera, and then he could see him, face filling Jack's phone screen.

"Can you see me, Jack? Yeah?" A smile. One like Jack had never wanted to punch so much. "Take a look."

The camera shook and spun, making Jack's stomach somersault. He saw Katie and Josh come into frame for a second, then the picture spun again, zooming to show a young man standing near Katie. He was pale, shaking, utterly terrified. Another spin, and the camera stopped on a young woman in a suit. Her face was contorted with grief and tears, and he could hear her sobs as they wracked her body. Finally, a dead man on the floor, throat ripped out, and leg missing below the knee.

"What have you done?"

The picture settled on Rich again. "It's not what we've done, Jack, it's what we *will* do."

10

Harry felt sick. The terror on this train, the panic their very presence engendered in the passengers felt so, so wrong. Rich and Chris were enjoying themselves too much. Being a figure of fear had never appealed to him – or at least, that's what he'd always told himself.

The reality was that Flo had saved him. Her love for him had pulled him back from the brink of self-destruction. Back, *before*, he'd been a gambler. Racking up a mountain of debt and then he'd found himself in a lockup in South London alone with a couple of guys with baseball bats.

He and Flo first met in school, had gone out for a bit, then drifted apart. She went radio silent on him after Year 13 and he had no idea why. There'd been rumours of an attack, which he'd dismissed – surely she'd have told him?

Turned out she *had* been attacked. Walking home from Harry's, already thinking about the next stage of her life, moving on to Uni, moving away and what would that mean for their relationship? She'd been so distracted with her thoughts she hadn't realised the shape coming towards her was a wolf, not a dog. When she saw it, her first thought had been to pet it and that saved her life. Didn't save her from a bite though. Didn't save her from the screaming pain in her arm, nor the horror of the wolf turning into a man. "Sorry," he'd said and burst into tears. Then he ran away, and she never saw him again. She passed out from the pain under a large bush, dense with foliage.

She woke the next day, wounded and hurt, but she went home anyway. Her mum assumed she'd been with Harry and never asked any questions. Flo knew what had happened to her, knew what it meant and so ghosted Harry.

As a teenage boy, coming out of his first proper relationship, Harry was devastated but he never forgot her. He found it close to impossible to look for a new relationship and started drinking heavily instead. As a regular in drinking holes, he soon got invited to card games. He won the first few games and won large. All a ploy to drag him in, of course, and as a drinker, he didn't realise until it was too late. By then, he owed six figures and had absolutely no way to pay, hence the alone time with the goons and their baseball bats.

Flo found him dumped in an alley. His arm was broken, cheekbone too. She nursed him back to health, kept him hidden from the debt collectors who were ready for more than a few broken bones. When she revealed her true nature, he leapt at the chance to change. Let those fuckers come at him now – they'd have a hell of a shock.

It was Flo who talked him round from that, made him realise that more violence wasn't the solution. *You can always walk away,* she'd say. They went on the road, moving from place to place, living under different names. All great practice, as it turned out, for a life on the run when the military started their crusade against wolves.

Back on the train, Harry knew that Rich's approach was all wrong. Stadler was never going to co-operate, even with a threat to his wife and kid. He knew they were poking a bear, but what could he do? Rich was in charge now, and no way could Harry confront him. Rich would destroy him in a one to one.

He couldn't walk away.

Not yet.

Flo would be so disappointed.

Equally, he didn't like how much Rich and Chris were enjoying it. He got the impression they would have, with or without wolf counterparts. Rich had the face of a hard life, lived harder. Beady eyes, a nose which had clearly been broken more than once, near-permanent scowl. Chris wasn't much better, but at least he'd been given the looks of the family. *Probably why he's so happy all the time.*

Chris's eyes were all over Katie Stadler and Harry didn't need to be a mind reader to know what he was thinking. Sure, she was a mum, and a bit older than Harry, but she was a fine-looking woman. It would be the work of moments to rush over there, tear her clo—

No.

Yes.

Harry gripped the headrest, fingers digging into the soft material, tearing it. He clenched his jaw hard enough for it to hurt. *NO.* He concentrated on memories of Flo: her smile; her easy laugh; the good she saw in everyone, no matter what; how she came back into his life like an angel.

She was a drug addict.

He could feel his heart hammering in his chest, feel the adrenaline coursing through him. His nostrils flared as he tried to control his breathing. Failing. Knew the wolf was moments away.

NO. NO. NO!

He turned away and saw Chris grinning at him. He could rip his throat out, *that* would wipe the fucking look off his face. And like that, Harry was back in control. He eased his grip of the headrest, his breathing back to normal.

Close.

Chris continued smirking at him. "Thought you were going then Harry, mate."

"Let's just get her and get going." Harry scowled, hoping Chris couldn't see his legs shaking and how white his knuckles were.

Katie watched him, with her arms around Josh. The boy also studied Harry with wide eyes, his face pale. Harry swallowed hard and turned his scowl on them until they looked away. Katie muttered something, like 'Don't look,' and stared out the window, lips pursed.

She wouldn't have looked at him like that if Flo were here. But then, they wouldn't *be* here if Flo was alive. What would she do in a situation like this? *Easy – not get in it in the first place.*

"Mrs Stadler, we don't want to hurt you, or your boy." It seemed like a good starting point.

"Then let us go." Katie pointed at Chris. "Get your fucking eyes off me."

Chris's grin broadened, and he made an even bigger deal of running his eyes over her body with a leer.

Rich laughed. He hung up and threw the phone over his shoulder. "Looks never hurt anyone," he said. "You need to come with us."

11

"My husband will kill you."

"Jack will help us."

"Mummy, who's Jack?"

"Not now honey."

Rich's eyes narrowed, a sly grin in place. "He doesn't know Daddy's real name, does he?"

"Fuck off." She tried to put defiance into the words, she really did.

"Such a potty mouth for a mother!" Rich made a big play of looking around the carriage, at his naked friends and the cowering passengers. "Tell me, does he know your real name?"

Katie blanched. Of course, they'd planned on telling Josh everything one day. Just not *today*.

"Time to go Mrs S. Up you get." Rich gripped her arm. His fingers dug into the flesh there and she winced. Katie made a fist and swung her arm, catching Rich by surprise. His head snapped to the side as the blow caught his jaw. The look on his face told her she'd made a tragic, horrible mistake.

He didn't loosen his grip not even for a second. His hand swung at a terrifying pace, smacking her cheek and raking across her face. Pain immediately bloomed behind her eyes and her head rang like a bell. She felt something warm trickle down her face, but then it was a stream. Her entire body trembled as her skin peeled away from her cheek and the blood became a river.

"Mum!"

"Jesus, Rich, what have you done?"

The last thing Katie heard was Rich growling as he opened his mouth, teeth growing to razor sharp points as his face elongated into a snout and he bit into her neck, tearing her throat out.

12

Harry's mouth dropped open as Katie Stadler's corpse hit the floor with a thud. Blood squirted from her neck, pulsing out with enough force to cover the seats where she had just sat.

"Rich, what the fuck?"

He made to grab Rich, but Chris's hand shot out. "Don't," he said.

Rich glanced at Harry, face normal now, apart from the blood smeared around his mouth and chest. "We don't need her," he said. He reached over the blood coated seat and dragged Josh into the carriageway. "Hello, little man."

"Jesus, Rich, he's just a kid."

"So were we once." He knelt down, ignoring the blood squelching under him. "Now, kiddo, we really don't want to hurt you."

Josh swung his fist and hit Rich on the nose. Tears streamed down his face. Chris laughed, and he hadn't let go of Harry's arm.

"One shot is all you get kid. You need to do better if you want to hurt me." Rich stood and shifted his grip to the boy's hair. "Now, you're coming with us. Chris?"

"Yeah?"

"Kill them all."

Rich tightened his grip on the boy's hair. He couldn't help it. He wasn't a violent man, but sometimes, *sometimes*—

13

The phone went dead. *What we will do.*

Jack stared at the handset, his head whirling through a million different options and emotions. At the centre of it all, popping back to the front of his thoughts:

I will kill you all if you hurt either of them.

Stupid, so stupid. Why did I send them away? Here he was, the most powerful Wolf in the land, possibly the world, and he'd sent his family away, where he couldn't protect them. If there was a picture of stupid in the dictionary, it looked like him.

Jack, we're in trouble. We love you.

He dialled a number, even as Bailey's headlights came into view at the bottom of the road. A number he hadn't dialled or even thought of in years. He waited for it to connect, knowing it would go to voicemail, but disappointed all the same. The message would get through, but he wished he could speak face to face.

A beep from the other end of the line. An automated voice saying the number and to leave a message.

"Knowles. I need your help."

Interlude - Huntleigh

1

1 month ago

Jordan grinned, blowing hair out of her mouth as she moved off him. Her cheeks flushed red, and her breathing was slowing. At moments like this, Alex couldn't believe how lucky he was. With her perfume heavy in the confined space of the car, he was overwhelmed by a sense of *her*.

He knew he didn't love her, or at least, he thought he didn't. Lust yes, oh god, definitely in lust with her. This had been a month-long thing and he didn't know how much longer it would last. He had a few months left on his posting, but what would happen then? *Make like Potter and get an extension.* The sarge was happy with his work (of course she was. He volunteered for extra slots so he could watch Jordan), so why not get an extension? It was easy work after all: just watch a bunch of civvies do their normal lives. Watch some trees blow in the wind.

The worst thing was lying to Jordan. Necessary, but awful all the same.

She shuffled back to the front of the car, slipping into the passenger seat. He pulled his jeans up and got into the front seat, quickly checking nothing had been left in the rear. It was Sandeman's car, and whilst he was pretty sure Jordan hadn't been the first naked woman back there, he didn't want to give Sandeman any cause to moan. She was really good at that.

"Next weekend, my mum is away," Jordan said, a mischievous glint in her eyes.

"Okay," he said, and she looked disappointed at his apparent lack of enthusiasm. How could he explain he didn't want his team mates to watch him shagging?

"We could actually be in a bed for once." She reached over and stroked the back of his head. "Think what we could do with a bit more room."

He had thought about it. Often. "I'll check my shifts."

"Get the night off," she said.

"I'll try." He gunned the engine, pulling out from the dirt track he'd found on one of his runs. *What the hell am I going to do?* He knew she was pouting, but maybe the reason she seemed to like him was his aloofness and the fact he played hard to get. *Yeah right. Hard to get, my arse. Just switch the fucking cameras off.*

It was not far to the pub, so he didn't have much time to put her mind at ease. "Hey, I'll work something out. Saturday right?"

She grinned at him, and his heart threatened to burst. Maybe it was love, after all.

2

Three weeks ago

"Anyone thought about what happens if we have a power cut?" Alex put the mugs of tea on the table. It was him, Sandeman, the sarge and Potter. Wijnberg and Howells were on the monitors upstairs with Sandeman and Potter having just finished their shift. Both looked tired and eager to leave.

"The genny will kick in," Potter said, stifling a yawn. "Didn't your read your briefing?"

"And if the generator isn't working?"

"Why wouldn't it work?" Another yawn.

For her part, Sandeman looked at the door with a sense of longing. "Lover boy wants to get some alone time."

"What?" Alex knew he was blushing.

"You think we haven't seen you with that Jordan Ploughman?" Sandeman smiled. "Although, I must say I approve of your choice."

"I—,"

"Leave it, Alex." Kenny said. "You want to sleep with her, you go ahead. We won't watch. Just be in her room and we'll turn the camera off."

"Yeah," Potter said. "Keep it in your pants till you get upstairs." He tapped Alex on the shoulder. "I'm going for a drink. Coming?" He directed this at Sandeman.

"Nah man, I got a date."

They both left, leaving Alex and Kenny with four hot mugs of tea.

"For fuck's sake," Kenny said, pushing one of the extra mugs to Alex. "Look, you know how this goes. We're here to watch, make sure no-one goes anywhere they shouldn't."

"I thought I'd be in trouble."

"Trouble? Jesus, Alex, of course not. This is a cushy assignment, and as long as we're vigilant it'll stay so."

"I guess."

"We all went through the same adjustment, Alex. Your predecessor wanted out because he was bored, that's all. Nothing more, nothing less." She drank from one of the mugs in great gulps. If she burnt her throat, she gave no indication. "When you're with her, just keep an eye on her mum, that's all I ask."

Alex frowned but nodded. From what he'd seen and heard, Jordan only ever had nice words for Emilia.

"Her mum?"

"Yeah, she's got a couple of brothers who are wrong 'uns. Captain Knowles is tracking them across the country but they've not been in touch with Ploughman senior as far as we can tell. When you're there, just look for any written messages – they're about all we can't check."

"Written messages? What like in the last century?"

Kenny's look would have cooled all the tea. "They may have received letters, you know, snail mail. Just keep your eyes open."

"Okay," Alex said, a sinking feeling in his stomach. Somehow, checking Emilia's mail seemed wrong, even though he spied on Jordan daily.

Kenny threw something else at him and he caught it, foil creasing in his hand. "And for fuck's sake, use protection."

3

One week ago

Alex ran down the hill to Jordan's house. The last two weeks had been a dream, X-rated ones at that. He grinned as he ran, his body feeling like it was on fire as he thought about what was ahead. Jordan undressing. Her smooth skin trembling under his fingers. Hell, his *own* skin doing the same under her touch.

Jordan yanked the door open as he arrived, grabbing his t-shirt and hauling him into the kitchen, hot lips on his already, with fingers tugging at his jeans.

Alex looked over her shoulder without breaking the kiss. He moved his hand up her back, and made a slashing gesture with it, eyes on the light fixture in the middle of the room. Then he lost himself to her touch.

4

Kenny saw the embrace, the kiss and Alex's 'cut' action. She sighed, smiling to herself. *Young love. What a thing.*

On the screens, she caught some movement. Was that Mrs Ploughman? *Well, you'd better be quick.* She laughed out loud at that. Like Alex was ever anything less than quick. However, she had no desire to see the young couple fuck, or for the inevitable arrival of Mrs Ploughman.

Alex could fill her in later. She flicked the feed from the Ploughmans' house off.

5

Flushed and sweating from exertion, Alex grinned as Jordan fished a couple of cold lagers out of the enormous fridge.

Her blouse hung loosely, giving him glimpses of her flesh every time she moved, and he thought it wouldn't be long before he was ready to go again. *God, this woman!*

She popped the bottle caps off and offered him one. They both drank greedily, maintaining eye contact over the bottles.

"That was fun," she said.

He grinned. "I was terrified your mum would walk in on us."

"Nah, mum's away for a couple of days. She'll be home later, but my shift'll have started then."

"So we're alone?"

"Oh yes." She grinned, and like that, they were all over each other again.

CHAPTER 8

1

Bailey found Jack on the doorstep to his flat. It couldn't have been more than five minutes since they'd parted company. Jack's agitation was clear from the way he tapped his feet and his arms hung loose by his sides like he didn't know what to do with them.

"They've got her. Fucking bastards, they've got her."

"Who, Jack?" Even though he'd always known Jack's real name, it still felt strange to say it.

"They've taken Katie and Josh. I'm going to—" He stopped, nostrils flaring, eyes wide, a hint of colour in his cheeks. "If they hurt either of them—" His face creased, tears forming in his eyes. *What? What exactly are you going to do? You haven't been in a fight for ten years.*

"Easy man, easy," Bailey said, hands out, palms forward. Jack's eyes flashed a different colour again. Blue. Yellow. Blue again. Bailey gritted his teeth and smoothed his hair away from his forehead. "Where are they?"

"The train. They're on the train."

"Come on then." Bailey led him to the car, retrieved the keys from their not-so-subtle hiding spot and floored the accelerator as the engine was back on. Whilst the train station was a half hour drive West, it then travelled East along the coast line before heading inland. Depending where it was, they were unlikely to catch up with it any time soon.

As they drove, Jack filled him in on what he knew, which was very little. Still, Bailey drove as fast as he dared, using all his training to keep them on the road. It had been years since he'd felt this level of adrenaline, but his reflexes remained good. *Muscle memory. When you need it, it comes back.* The words of his drill sergeant, as clear now as the day he'd said them, as justification for the umpteenth time they'd completed the same task over and over.

Military life: ninety nine percent of the time spent bored shitless or working out and training, one percent in abject terror for your life. As he drove, it all came flooding back and he embraced the adrenaline rush, leant into it. He felt alive in a way he hadn't since quitting to become a teacher. Sure, teaching was a great job, but it never made you feel alive like *this*. Getting year nine to play football or rugby was not the same rush as chasing a fucking train.

They roared down the road, which was still quiet although it wouldn't be for much longer. The train cut East along the coast before heading South to Aberdeen, then across to Edinburgh. From what Jack had said, the train was stuck in the middle of nowhere, so they hadn't reached Aberdeen yet.

Jack also said there was no background noise; no clackety clack of wheel on tracks.

They'd been driving nearly an hour when they saw lights in a field ahead. The train. Stationary, like Jack said.

"There." Bailey pointed and pulled over by a hedge near the line. They both got out, standing at the edge of the road. The train was clear on the tracks ahead, with a deep, dark wood behind it. Jack jumped a gate in the hedge, entering the field.

"Hold up!" Bailey called, before opening the boot and retrieving his weapon. A G17, nine in the mag, little in the way of recoil. In Bailey's opinion, a great weapon, but it looked a little underpowered for what they might be about to face.

Jack ignored him, running across the field towards the train line.

"Shit," Bailey said and gave chase, wishing he had the heft of an SA80 with him. He couldn't get anywhere near Jack, despite the good shape he kept himself in. Jack was too fast.

"Can you smell that?" Jack shouted without slowing.

"What?"

"Blood."

2

"Wait," Bailey said.

They slowed when they reached the tracks at the front of the train. It had a small room for the driver, and Jack could see clearly into it. Blood coated the windows of all three carriages.

"Where is everyone?" Bailey said. "Someone must have survived."

Jack didn't say anything, just stood with his head bowed. *These are my people. This is what we do.*

Gripping his weapon more tightly, Bailey approached the driver's compartment. The door swung open, banging in the latch. He nearly tripped over something, and when he looked down, he saw the mutilated remains of the driver. Bailey doubled over and threw up, wet vomit splashing over a rock resting against one of the rails.

"Shit," he said and wiped his mouth with the back of his hand. "Sorry."

Jack blanched when he saw the corpse but didn't throw up. He didn't say anything, moving towards the train. Bailey put a hand on his chest and held up his Glock. Jack gave a wan smile and showed his teeth.

Bailey made an 'after you' gesture, pulling himself up using the handrail with one hand as soon as Jack entered the compartment. The other kept the G17 ready. His hand shook – a small tremor, but a tremor, nonetheless.

Jack pulled the door to the carriage open, and it banged in its frame like the external door. The scene it revealed looked like the worst bits of the Bible.

"Holy fuck," Bailey said.

His weapon was unnecessary, that much was clear. Everyone in the carriage was dead. Some of them were missing limbs, but most were eviscerated. Stomachs ripped open, or rib cages, or both. Entrails hung over the back of seat and the bodies were all in the aisle, apart from one next to the door. In their panic, everyone had tried to run and been cut down in the process.

Jack looked at the corpse, seeing what would have been a young woman. Her severed head was on the seat next to her, like it was placed there rather than falling. She still had her headphones in. Blood coated the floor, windows and ceiling around her. *First to die, or at least, first after the driver.* He could see how it unfolded. They'd stopped the train, probably using the rock outside. Someone had come out to move it and let the wolves onto the train.

Everything after that would have been quick. When this woman died, the rest of the passengers would have panicked, fear rolling down the carriage like a wave. With nowhere to run to except further back along the train, the outcome would never have been in doubt.

The nausea was back with a vengeance, and this time he had no choice but to give in to it. Vomit splashed over the blood-soaked floor and Jack doubled over, heaving to get it all out. He straightened, wiping his mouth with the back of his hand with a shudder.

"Look at this." Bailey's face was as red as Jack's was pale. He was trembling, his Glock held with white knuckles by his side.

"Bailey, I—"

"Don't tell me you didn't do this. Don't. Look around, Jack, look at it!"

Jack was looking, and more vomit threatened to spill out. Underneath, though, there, *there* was the Wolf, straining to come out. *Smell it, Jack. Oh, how glorious! I've missed this. You've missed it. Come on, let me out, cut loose.*

"Bailey, you need to go."

"Is that a threat? Are you fucking threatening me?"

Jack shook his head. "I didn't do this Bailey."

"No, maybe not directly. But your *kind* did."

And there it was. It wouldn't matter how innocent Jack was, he would forever be inseparable from this.

"Calm down, Bailey. I'm not your enemy." Jack waited for a response, hoping the barrel wouldn't end up pointing at him. When it didn't move, he continued, "Not all wolves are like this, come on, man, you've watched me for years – you know."

Bailey held Jack's gaze, tears spilling from his eyes. He took a few rapid breaths, but it didn't seem to help him calm down. "Fuck." It was woefully inadequate.

"I need to find my wife and my son," Jack said, pushing past Bailey and heading down the carriage, taking care to step over bodies and body parts. The smell of blood made the Wolf growl inside. Jack ignored it: at least he could still do that. *But for how much longer Jack? Mmmmm, I'm hungry Jack....*

The second carriage was the same, but with less bodies. People had figured out they were in trouble by this point, had more time to flee. When he reached the final carriage, he saw that wasn't true. Five people dead in here, all ripped apart. *Christ, what a mess.*

He made his way along the carriage, examining each body for a few seconds as he went. None of the corpses were small enough to be Josh, but Katie—

No.

He refused to let his thoughts go down that route. They wouldn't kill Katie if they wanted his help. It would be a death sentence for them. He knew that. They knew that. He hoped.

One of the bodies caught his eye. Blue jeans, t-shirt that would have been white once but was now nearly black with blood. Something glinted to his left and he reached for it. A mobile phone, tossed to one side. Same make as Katie's. He tapped the screen and a picture of him and Josh came into view, both smiling and holding a massive salmon. Tears swam in his eyes, blurring the picture. He dropped the phone and moved closer to the dead woman.

His hand shook as he reached towards the corpse in the aisle. He already knew, of course he did, but he had to be sure. There was always hope – until you were sure.

"Jack," Bailey said, retrieving the phone. His face was ashen.

Jack flipped the body over and the air rushed out of him. His legs crumbled under him, and he fell to the floor, an anguished cry falling from him. The world around him – the carnage, the death, the smell – all faded to insignificance.

"Fuck," Bailey said.

Let me out Jack. I'll kill everyone for you. My gift.

Jack hugged her corpse – still warm – and sobbed. He rocked back and forth as if that would give her life back. As he did so, the Wolf chattered on in his head, imploring him, begging him to be let out. Jack ignored it, consumed by his grief.

3

A helicopter roared overhead, it's engines loud and drowning out Jack's cries. Bailey craned his neck to look out of the window, eyes on the sky. The helicopter was black against the brightening sky as it circled the train, then began its descent to the field below.

Knowles.

The phone buzzed in his hand, dragging his attention from the approaching helicopter. A message came into view, a flash preview on the lock screen.

We have your son. Leave us alone and he lives.

The message was showing as having an attachment. Bailey unlocked the phone by typing in the code with a shaking hand and tapped on the message. A picture. Josh, alive but scared, stuffed into what looked like the rear seat of a small car.

Above the message, a single word showed as the sender.

Josh.

"Shit, Jack, look at this!"

Jack ignored him, not making eye contact.

"Jack. It's Josh, they have Josh."

4

Soldiers fanned out in an arc, backs to the helicopter, weapons aimed at the train. A quick scramble following Bailey's call left the team feeling tired and cranky. Jack's subsequent call only hardened the knot of anxiety building in his stomach. Knowles stood at the centre, lips a thin line. This didn't feel good at all.

I need your help.

The last time Jack Stadler needed his help, they'd both been lucky to escape with their lives. Many people hadn't. Another day when his entire team got killed. Another day *he* survived. Maybe Towner was right to question why he always survived.

Lucky, just bloody lucky.

Still, he didn't feel lucky standing in this field, with the sun only just clear of the horizon. It was cold even with the adrenaline coursing through him. He supposed it might get warmer later, but well, it *was* Scotland.

The train sat just ahead, no sign of movement inside. The driver's door hung open, inviting people aboard. At the far end of the train, a smashed window looked to be the only other external damage. As they moved closer, he could see splashes of something over the windows and it took a couple more steps before he realised it was blood.

Of course its blood. Here we go again.

A corpse lay next to the tracks. From the uniform, it had once been the driver.

"Sir?" Towner looked over at him, holding position and covering the open doorway in front of him. Miller was next to him, but Towner ignored him. Miller frowned, the expression dragging his wounds upwards. He was going to have some decent scars.

Could be a problem, that.

"Proceed with caution, Towner. Miller, you've got point."

Miller clambered into the open doorway without any hesitation. *Good.* Knowles wanted the young man to do well; wanted him to overcome the fear from the last mission. He needed a *team*.

"Clear." Miller's voice, shattering the silence of the field. Towner scrambled onto the train, and he and Miller moved further along the carriage, blood-stained windows obscuring their progress.

Knowles stayed in the field with Penfold. Seconds became minutes as the men made their way along the carriages. A few shouts, then they saw three indistinct shapes come back along the carriage.

"Ready," Knowles said, drawing his pistol. Penfold raised her weapon, but they both relaxed when they saw Miller and Towner with a third man.

Bailey jumped off the train and nodded at Knowles. "Been a while, sir."

Knowles shook his hand. "You know you don't need to call me that anymore."

"Hard habit to break."

"How bad is it?"

Bailey took a moment before answering. He was a little heavier than when he'd left the service, a bit of a spread across his midriff, a hint of a double chin, but overall, he looked pretty good. His eyes were as sharp as ever, even if his face was pale. *He has seen some shit today.*

"Bad. No survivors." A tremor in his voice, then a pause, before, "None."

"Where's Jack?"

Towner's lip curled at the name.

Bailey jerked a thumb over his shoulder, pointing at the last train carriage. "He's not in a good way, sir."

Knowles took no satisfaction from the other man's unease. Despite being news around the world for a while all those years ago, stories of wolves faded. Lots of websites had been dedicated to wolf sightings originally, but they lost their followings, lost advertising, lost relevance. Newer ones took their place, dismissing it all as a hoax. It suited

Knowles to let them drift: his job was much easier without Joe Public ringing the helpline every thirty seconds.

I think my neighbour is a wolf....

I saw one last night...

There's a dead bird in my garden, it might be a wolf....

That was one of the more ridiculous ones and easily dismissed. Like a sparrow could feed one of these monstrosities. Katie Stadler had said to him not all wolves were bad. Knowles had been angry then, furious at the loss of life, but he'd come around to her way of thinking. Some of these people just wanted a simple life. Pre-Jack, they'd had no idea wolves even existed. Wolves were good at keeping themselves hidden. *Had been*, he corrected himself.

His policy now was to leave wolves alone. Keep them quiet, out of the public eye. He only tracked proven dangerous ones, like the pair in London. *And what a shitshow that turned out to be.* Maybe it was time to have a new policy. *No, get the targets. The ones that started this, then let Jack get back to anonymity.*

It bothered him that Jack was involved. How did they know about him? It had been ten years – did he still carry that weight with the wolves? That notoriety? How had they found him? What did this massacre on the train mean?

"Sir." Bailey's voice cut through his thoughts, dragging him back to the field.

"Just call me Knowles."

Bailey nodded, and for the first time, Knowles noticed how pale he was. "We can get you some help, Bailey."

Bailey looked confused at that. "Sir, it's bad on the train, but um, well—," he paused, breathing deeply, knowing his voice had just cracked.

"Spit it out Bailey."

"Katie's dead, sir. They killed her."

"Who killed her?" Knowles' stomach lurched. Had Jack finally snapped? Why now? After all this time? He was devoted to his wife, so what the hell?

"Some guys turned up at our local. Threatened Jack. They called him from the train a little while ago. Couple of brothers and some other guy."

Knowles's gut twisted again at the *couple of brothers*. "Why was Katie on the train? Do you know?"

"Jack sent her and Squiggs away. Guess the other guys anticipated that move."

"Squiggs?"

Bailey's cheeks flushed red. "Josh, sir."

"Right."

"Everyone else is dead, sir. No survivors on the train at all."

Behind him, Towner nodded. Miller looked like he was going to be sick.

"They have Josh, sir. I have Katie's phone."

"What's on the phone?"

"It'll be locked, sir." Towner really was proving to be an irritating shit.

"Luckily, I know the code," Bailey said, matching Towner's smug tone.

"You did take spying seriously then?" Knowles said.

"Not really, but it's not hard. It's Squigg's birthday." Bailey tapped on the screen and held it up so Knowles could see. A photo filled the frame.

"This was about an hour ago. Christ knows where they are now."

"Local police en route, sir," Penfold said. She'd been monitoring the police band, listening for any message about the train.

"Good. This isn't going to break well. Inform them we are dealing with it, and they need to let us do our job." He ran a hand through is hair. "We need APB's out on these guys, with a do not approach warning."

Penfold frowned but saluted. "Yes sir."

"Problem?"

"No sir."

Knowles sighed. "Penfold, we're a small team. If you have a problem, spit it out."

Penfold glanced at Towner. "No problem, sir."

"Ok, Miller, with me and Bailey. Let's go. Weapons ready."

CHAPTER 9

1

Jack pushed himself into a sitting position, throat raw from crying.

Katie lay next to him, blood covering her. Her eyes were open, staring at him, no, *through* him. Focussed on nothing at all. He reached out, touching her face, ignoring the sticky mess of blood there.

He stared at her, willing her to life, but of course, nothing happened. A cold, numb feeling spread through him, radiating out from his stomach. Tears filled his eyes and he tried to blink them away, but failed. He curled into the foetal position as his whole body shook. *You can't heal this.*

He didn't want to look at her again, wanted instead to remember her as she'd been. The resolute smile, the beautiful eyes full of love for him and Josh. He wanted to remember the warmth of her touch, the way his skin felt electric every single time she touched him. It was something he'd always thought would fade over their marriage, but hadn't. He wanted to remember her laugh, but right then he couldn't – the sight in front of him consumed all thoughts.

He wailed, then, a long, agonised scream escaping him until he was out of breath. Even if he'd been there, she wouldn't have wanted him to heal her. She'd never wanted to be a wolf, had never wanted his powers. His Wolf half had always disgusted her, even if she'd never voiced the thoughts. He had killed a doctor in front of her, years ago. Absolutely obliterated the poor man before Jack learned how to control the Wolf. He wasn't sure she'd ever really forgiven him for all the months she'd thought he was dead.

Don't be ridiculous. She loved you.

Completely.

Utterly.

Never, ever, doubt that.

The last few thoughts came in her voice, and he wailed again. Every fibre of him hurt, and yet he also felt dead inside. An emptiness opened deep inside, and the Wolf poured in.

2

Knowles and Miller crept closer to the train, SA80s ready. Bailey brought up the rear, his face pale. The noise coming from the train didn't sound good. Someone sounded in great pain, and Knowles knew it was Jack.

He led the way into the first carriage, pausing in the doorway as the scene revealed itself in all its horrifying glory. He held up two fingers and pointed forward, indicating Miller where should move to.

Miller obeyed, barely making a sound despite the gear he carried. He kept his SA80 trained along the length of the carriage as he went. Knowles was impressed: the young man remained focussed on his job, despite the gruesome surroundings.

Bailey drew level with Knowles, his handgun shaking. *He's been out of the game too long.* Despite this, Bailey moved like he had forgotten none of his training, which was the first bit of good news Knowles had received today.

Miller moved to the second carriage.

3

Jack smelt them long before they reached him. A familiar scent – *Bailey* – and someone else. The Wolf bared its teeth inside, and he felt its hairs bursting out along his arms.

No.

He knew he was losing. Knew there was nothing he could do. His grief was too great and the Wolf had found the weakness it needed to escape it's cage.

Even as it overwhelmed him, he found his voice, long enough for one word. He opened his mouth and screamed.

"RUN!"

4

Bailey heard the shout as Miller reached the end of the second carriage. He recognised Jack's voice, even though it sounded strange, like he'd put it through some sort of voice changer.

"Wait!"

Miller either didn't hear him or chose not to. He took a step forward, and a huge shape smashed into him knocking him backwards into Bailey. As he fell, his finger squeezed the trigger sending bullets flying wild into the wall, windows and seats near him. The noise echoed off the walls, deafening them to everything except the Wolf's roar.

Bailey could see the Wolf clearly. It was much larger than a wolf should be, covered in brown fur tinged with streaks of white. *Same as Jack, it's the same as Jack.* Warm piss rolled down his leg at the sight of it this close to him. The barrel of the Glock shook and Bailey staggered backwards, trying to put as much distance between himself and it as possible.

The Wolf lowered its head, towards Miller and sniffed him. Miller screamed, but then the Wolf turned its malevolent gaze to Bailey and growled. Bailey turned to run, a low moan escaping his lips as he moved, even though he knew the futility of running. The Wolf would close the distance between them in a couple of bounds, open its terrible jaws and—

Knowles aimed and fired.

Bullets tore into the creature, punching holes into its side the size of a fist. It howled as its rear legs collapsed. Knowles continued to fire as he walked forward, towards the Wolf. Bailey wanted to shout at him, tell him to get away, but Knowles wasn't in the mood to listen. More bullets flew into the Wolf, pushing it back off Miller until finally it collapsed to the carriage floor unmoving.

"Yes!" Bailey yelled.

"You fucking idiot," Knowles said. It wasn't entirely clear if he was talking to Miller or Bailey.

Miller stood, frantically checking himself for bites and wounds. He looked like he was doing some bizarre combination of the Macarena and having a fit.

"Tie him up," Knowles said, drawing Miller's attention from the Wolf.

"Sir?"

"You heard. Tie him up." He looked into the final carriage. "Bailey, with me."

5

Knowles surveyed the horrible mess of blood, limbs and innards and felt a familiar sickness wash over him. *Fucking wolves.* He saw Katie's corpse and ran a hand through his hair. Knowles checked her pulse, despite the huge amount of blood, the open, unstaring eyes and the pale flesh. He knew it was a futile gesture, but he had to check. Had to know. "I'm so sorry," he said, voice barely above a whisper.

He remembered Katie telling him, a long time ago, not all wolves were bad. She was using Jack as an example, but she was trying not to go for hate, even back then. Had she still felt like that, as her blood drained away? Had she had time to recognise the sheer terror these horrific creatures spread?

"We need to find Josh," Bailey said.

It took Knowles a moment to realise who he was talking about. "They won't get far. Three naked blokes with a young kid would get some attention wherever they go."

Bailey nodded, but he was pale.

Knowles nodded at his trousers. "There's no shame in that you know?"

Colour burst in Bailey's cheeks. "Pretty fucking embarrassing, sir, not gonna lie."

"I had pretty much the same experience first time I saw him change." The lie was meant to be kind, but Bailey didn't look convinced.

"How the hell am I going to explain to Squiggs both his parents died tonight?"

"Both?" Knowles shook his head. "Did you even read the file I gave you?" He looked at Bailey with surprise. "Now we have a really, really pissed off Wolf to deal with."

Back in carriage two, the situation was almost comical. Miller hopped from foot to foot, eyes so wide they threatened to pop out of his head as he aimed his weapon at a naked Jack Stadler.

Jack's hands and feet were tied behind him and he knelt in front of Miller.

"Don't fucking move!" Miller roared, over and over.

Jack glowered at him but seemed sensible enough to be listening. Knowles held his own SA80 loosely, ready to use it if necessary. He glanced at Bailey, hoping he would realise Jack could be free of the bonds and on them before Miller blinked.

"Untie me Knowles."

"You going to play nice?"

"With you?" Jack's voice was still too deep, eyes too yellow. "Yes."

"You scared us a bit there, Jack. You nearly took Miller's head off." Knowles said.

"Jack—" Bailey started but couldn't finish. His voice broke and he stopped, looking away.

Jack stood, flexing his muscles, breaking the ropes and looming over Miller suddenly. The younger man shrieked as Jack batted the weapon away. All three soldiers took a step back from him, Bailey and Knowles aiming at Jack. "I need to find my son."

"Leave this to us," Knowles said. "Don't want to do anything stupid."

Jack's glare made them all freeze. "Stupid?" He snorted. "I'm going to find the men who kidnapped my boy and killed my wife."

"Jack—"

He shook his head, eyes still yellow. "None of them live, Knowles. None of them. I will fucking bury them all."

Chapter 10

1

The motorway was long and boring. Harry tried to stretch, but the steering wheel was in the way. He yawned instead, shifted his weight and kept his eyes on the road ahead. This was a different car than the one they'd left the train in. A Mazda of some description, but it was small. Probably what would be referred to as a 'run-around' or a 'car for the missus' by some dodgy dealer.

The four of them were a tight fit. Josh didn't take up any space, but the bulk of Rich and Chris cramped the insides. Chris had found the car on the edge of an estate just outside Inverness, parked outside an empty house. Now with fresh clothes, nicked from a washing line near where they'd found the car, they had a small window before the car would be reported stolen but should have a good few hours before they had to switch again.

Harry had the radio on, tuning out the DJs and bland music – why did everyone sound the same these days? He chuckled at the thought: when had he turned into such a middle-aged nobhead? Hell, he wasn't even that old.

As they drove past Manchester, Devon still felt a long way off. He pressed the accelerator.

"Slow down," Rich said, without bothering to open his eyes.

Harry's eye twitched. *How does he do that?*

"Don't draw attention to us."

Harry watched cars roar past them and then an articulated lorry. *Driving this slowly with make us look suspicious.* Of course, he didn't vocalise that thought. Antagonising Rich wasn't high on his list of things to do today. He had to keep him calm and rational until he had an opening to rescue the boy.

He could see him every time he looked in the rear-view mirror. His light brown hair, dark eyes and small nose meant he would be a good-looking boy when he grew up. If. *A proper heartbreaker,* Flo would say. Harry had to do everything he could to make sure Josh would see that future.

For now, the boy slept, exhausted from sobbing, his head pressed against the window. He twitched occasionally, and Harry had no desire to know his thoughts and dreams. *No kid should see their mother killed. Especially like that.*

And for what? As a test from Rich? Harry thought of the events on the train and shuddered. What had Rich been doing? Jack Stadler now had two reasons to come after them – to rescue his boy and for revenge. Harry didn't know which would lead to more trouble for them.

A dead woman. A kidnapped kid. *Fuck.*

As the miles dribbled past, he thought of Gary: he'd claimed to be healed by Jack, but he hadn't been an Original. He was, after all, dead – something really difficult to do to an Original. Was Jack truly an Original? Callum had believed so, all those years ago when he led an ill-fated assault on an army base. If he wasn't, then maybe Rich could kill him. That would be one way out of this mess, at least. If he was, then—

Harry didn't want to think about what would happen if Jack ever caught up with them.

Harry tried to blank out his thoughts and just drive.

"Here," Rich said, pointing at a sign indicating an approaching service station. "Time to switch cars."

2

Stealing a car was easy. They waited, watching the car park until a battered old CRV pulled in. A man in his fifties got out, stretching and headed straight to the service station. Chris watched as he went to the toilet, then headed for a breakfast in the main café. The guy, like a proper twat, put his phone and keys on a table, under a newspaper then joined the long queue for breakfast.

His keys were in Chris's pocket in seconds, and he headed back outside.

Rich, Harry and Josh got out of their car as soon as he approached, and they headed for the CRV. Chris yanked open the door to the car and bundled Josh into the back seat. The boy struggled, but it was no use, Chris was just too strong. Josh hit his head on the far door, and he cried out.

"Shut your mouth," Chris snarled. Josh stared at him, big eyes welling with tears. "And cut that out or I'll give you something to cry about."

As soon as he said it, he remembered those words coming from his father's mouth. Of course, they'd already been hit at least once by then and possibly more if he'd been drinking. If Chris had been more in tune with his emotions, he might have reflected on how his father's nurture – or lack of – had led to the life he currently had. He might have seen how his father's actions influenced his own.

But Chris had none of that. He knew his strength got him places, even before he was a wolf, and as long as he and Rich were together, nothing too bad would ever happen to either of them. His brawn, Rich's brains – that was all either of them needed. Of course, Rich's propensity for violence, and ability to do thing other people just wouldn't, helped.

Chris sat next to Josh, squashing him against the door. The boy wriggled for a moment, trying to push past Chris. He laughed, slapping the kid until he got the message and stopped.

Rich sat in the driver's seat, a grim smile on his face when Harry got in next to him.

"Still with us Harry?" Rich's smirk was punch worthy.

"Nowhere else for me." Harry was pale, but he had no fight or argument within him. He could run, yes, but that would mean leaving the kid with these arseholes. "Where are we going?"

Rich's smile widened. "Our sister has a place. The sprog might be able to help."

"Fucking A," Chris said.

"What?" Harry said, but Rich dismissed him with a wave.

"Let's go. I want to be in Devon by tonight."

3

Jack sat on the grass in the field next to the train tracks, holding Katie's hand, silent since his outburst. He'd carried her outside, not wanting her to spend a second longer surrounded by the carnage.

Knowing he could do nothing to help, Knowles left him to it. His team were liaising with the police, monitoring cars on the roads heading south. This was almost certainly futile as no-one knew what car they were in, but they might get lucky. *Yeah right. When have you ever been lucky with wolves involved?* Every stolen car report would be investigated thoroughly, probably a huge surprise for the people reporting the crime.

In the past, they would have hidden this sort of event from the public. A train crash. A freak gas explosion. Something along those lines. Knowles wanted people to know though – it was time to bring the fear of the wolves back to the population. He didn't want the guys holding Josh to have any safe harbour.

Knowles accepted a hot mug of tea from Towner, blowing on it and taking a grateful sip. Towner made to drink from his own mug, but Knowles held out his hand. In response to his frown, Knowles gestured at Jack with his head. Towner's shoulders sagged, but he handed the tea to Knowles anyway.

Knowles made his way to Jack, sitting next to him and holding the tea up. "Thought you could use this."

Jack's face was a picture of contempt.

"Seriously, you need this."

Jack took the mug, his face softening. "I can't believe this."

Knowles nodded. "Me neither. It's a shit show."

"I should have killed those men the moment they showed up in the pub."

"You weren't to know."

"I did though. I did know. It's my fault she was on that train." His face creased, and fresh tears fell.

Knowles kept quiet. He'd been around grief – hell, had even felt its grip on his own shoulders more times than he cared to remember – and knew there were no easy or quick solutions. Sudden unexpected death was always worse and even as a soldier he'd never got used to it.

You had to move on, deal with it in your own time. *No wonder so many ex-military were fucked up when they left.*

Instead of saying something crass, he kept quiet and sipped his tea. His thoughts didn't settle on anything in particular but cycled round the close friends he had lost over the years. The last team he had been truly close to had been the guys he'd been in Afghanistan with. Carruthers. Meyers. Scarlet. Jonesy. Men who had survived Helmand only to die back home in the UK.

Would they still be alive without Jack Stadler?

It was a question he had asked many times over the years. They'd been assigned to watch him in Devon, a mission in which Scarlet and Meyers lost their lives. Scarlet had been eaten by a wolf right in front of Knowles, but Meyers –

Knowles shuddered at the memory of spiders crawling all over a cave just before he buried it. He hadn't been there when Meyers died. Hundreds of the fucking things had bitten him when they'd retrieved bones from an ancient cave. The bones that had made Jack Stadler the way he was now. The bones that really had started all this. Knowles didn't understand the whys of how Jack had become an Original from being impaled on a bone, didn't understand the power of it all from how it healed to how it created these monsters, but he recognised the threat. The bones were back in Devon now, buried in the cave system where no-one could gain access to them. Knowles had made sure of that with a lot of explosives.

No more Originals. Thank fuck.

Would the wolves have attacked or become as brazen without wanting Jack as a figurehead? Knowles doubted it. From what he'd seen, most wolves wanted to just get on with their lives. Very few wanted to change the status quo – especially since their decimation in Kent. A huge battle leading to the deaths of lots of good people.

Carruthers. Jones. Claire Biddlestone. Even that monumental prick Smith. About the only good thing to come out of that shitshow was just how many wolves died that day.

It should have been enough to send the wolves scurrying back underground, but then, Bryant turned himself into an Original. *Bryant. Jesus. The ghosts are coming out today.* Bryant used the Original's bones to cure his cancer, which worked, but given Bryant had anger issues, adding wolf into the mix really didn't help. Another pack of wolves came out of the woodwork, and lots more good people died.

At the centre of it all, Jack Stadler. Some kind of Wolf God.

And now this. A dead woman and a missing child. All started because these men had found where Jack lived. Maybe he should put a bullet in Jack now and be done with it all. He might need Jack with these wolves who'd already proved themselves more cunning than he'd first thought.

Towner came back over and handed him a tablet with a photo on it. "This just came in. The pub where Stadler and Bailey went for a pint had CCTV in the car park. Shitty quality, as you'd expect, but it's definitely him."

Knowles saw the photo and swore. "Thanks, Towner."

Towner handed the tablet over, then left Knowles with Jack.

"Who?"

It took a moment for Knowles to realise Jack had spoken, so soft was his voice.

"Who are you talking about?"

Knowles sighed. This conversation would not go well. "The man who took Josh is someone we've been tracking. We lost him in London."

"Who?"

Knowles showed Jack the grainy picture of Harry and Rich. He pointed at Rich. "This man."

"Rich." Jack's voice was empty of emotion, but his eyes flashed yellow as he spoke.

"Yeah. Not a good man."

"What do you know about him?"

Knowles put the tablet down and sipped his tea. It was lukewarm. "Look, you know we've been hunting the wolves for years, right?"

Jack shrugged. "I heard bits and pieces, but I was keeping my head down."

"Sometimes your name comes up," Knowles said. "Not that often, but when it does it sends up a few red flags." He pointed at Rich, pressing the screen so a kaleidoscope of colour blurred around his fingertip. "This guy and his brother. They asked a lot. We've been tracking them."

"Why didn't you stop him?"

"We were always two steps behind. We got some intel from a woman called Flo. Know her?"

Jack shook his head.

"Said she was worried about some men, told us the location." Knowles sighed. "We were too late, Jack. Turned up to a flat in London and it went spectacularly wrong. They got away. People died. You know how it is. Some recently registered the flat in the name Gary Clarke."

Jack closed his eyes and breathed deeply, trying not to cry again.

"You knew him?"

"Knew?"

"He's dead."

"You sure?"

"We took his head off and burnt the remains." Knowles shrugged. "Pretty sure."

Jack filled him in. Cancer. Healed because he could and because Katie asked him to. "I had to send him away."

"Why?"

"Couldn't risk another Bryant situation. Couldn't control myself around Bryant – we'd just attack each other. Remember? Imagine that happening at my house?"

Knowles nodded, cogs turning. Silence hung heavy between them.

"Will you help me find them?"

Knowles nodded. "We'll get them Jack, but you need to stay out of it."

"They have my son. They killed my wife."

Throughout, Jack hadn't let go of Katie's hand. His eyes were red raw – even when they flashed yellow – and his foot tapped an irregular rhythm on the ground. Now his jaw clenched.

"They die, Knowles, simple as. You're either with me on this or –"

"Don't finish that sentence, Jack. I have a well of sympathy for you, but it's not bottomless."

They stared at each other, silence stretching until Jack broke it by crying again.

"She's dead, Knowles, she's dead and Josh is gone and it's all my fault."

4

"Don't do it to yourself Jack," Knowles said. "That shit'll eat you up."

Jack ignored him and continued to stroke Katie's hair. His foot still tapped the same irritating, irregular rhythm, and he kept his gaze locked on a spot on the floor in front of him. In his head, he saw Katie smiling at him, her eyes sparkling in the summer sun.

Let me out Jack. Let me do this for you. For us.

He shook his head, feeling the change happen and biting down hard on it. *No.* Out of the corner of his eye, he saw Knowles shy away from him, the empty mug left on the floor, reaching for his weapon.

For her.

His inner voice knew it had made a mistake. Jack was back in control in a second.

Don't mention her. Do not talk about her. She'd still be alive if it weren't for you.

Is that true though, Jack? Is it?

He didn't want to answer the question. Instead, he looked at Knowles, holding his hands up – the first time he had let go of her body.

"It's okay, Knowles, it's not coming out."

"You sure? It bloody looked like it." Knowles' hand was still near his SA80, although he wasn't holding it. Not yet.

"It wants revenge. At least, that's what it's telling me, but not yet, Knowles. Not until I'm with them." Jack stood at last, his legs trembling under him. "Have you found them?"

Knowles shook his head. "It's going to take time, Jack. They'll have switched vehicles. They could be anywhere."

Jack growled in frustration, and Knowles felt his legs go weak. Yes, this man was supposedly a friend, but nothing changed the fact he could rip Knowles apart before he really knew what was happening.

"Easy now, Jack. We'll get them. Right now, we need to get some food in you, okay?"

"I don't want to eat, Knowles."

Was his voice deeper again? Knowles picked up the SA80, no longer keeping his movements subtle.

"Well, I need to, so I'm going to get some scran." Without another word, he walked out of the room, leaving Jack behind.

Jack looked at Katie again, drinking in her face. "I'll find them," he said. "I swear to you, I'll get our son back."

5

The sun was high in the sky, and Knowles shielded his eyes from the glare. Towner sat in the helicopter, tapping away at a laptop. Miller and Penfold were cooking field rations over a camping stove a few metres away.

Penfold raised her arm in greeting as soon as she saw him. "Grub up in five, sir," she called.

He nodded and went to Towner. "How we doing?"

"Nothing yet. Won't be long though, right? Every copper in the country has their description."

"Yeah, but that worries me a little."

"How so, sir?"

Was Towner warming to him now? "Last thing we need is some wannabe hero plod trying to take them on."

"Plod? No-one says that anymore, sir." Towner failed to suppress a laugh. "You sound like my granddad."

A flush of heat ran across Knowles' cheeks, but he forced a chuckle out. "Your grandad must be a pretty cool bloke."

"Well, he's dead, so there's that."

Knowles clenched his teeth until his jaw hurt. "Check in with the Huntleigh crew, please."

"Sir? They checked in two days ago. Not due another check till oh-eight hundred tomorrow."

"Just do it." Knowles walked away, leaving Towner muttering to himself. He knew he should turn back and chew the younger man out, but right then, he was too angry. Or was it scared? Knowles shook his head, not caring how it would look to anyone watching him. Jack worried him. Grief did terrible things to a person, as did anger. Combined?

Sure, he could let Jack take out his anger on the brothers. Take a step back and let him tear them limb from limb, but would it end there? Would Jack be able to regain control? *No guarantees, Knowles, no guarantees.*

Interlude - Huntleigh

1

2 days ago

"Can't believe her mum didn't walk in on you," Kenny said.

Alex pulled his coat on. His shift was over, with the sarge about to take over. Downstairs, Potter and Sandeman were cooking a huge chilli for them all. Howells and Wijnberg were due back any time, but this was the first time in a few days his shift had coincided with Kenny's.

"What do you mean?"

"The other day, when you asked me to turn the cameras off. Jordan's mum was in the pantry. I was tempted to keep watching to see the fireworks." Kenny laughed. "You and the prodigal daughter, going at it and she walks in, classic."

He frowned. "Nah, sarge, it's alright. Her mum was away, but she's back now. Later." Without another word, he walked out, his shift over which meant he was only going to one place.

Kenny watched him go, frowning. *What the hell?* She turned to the bank of computers and pulled up the archive of the previous week. It had been a while since she'd had to review files, and it took a couple of minutes to find the right file. She flew through it, fast enough for it to look comical but slow enough to still see details.

There.

Alex and Jordan, pawing at each other's clothes. She noted the timestamp and pulled up the pantry cameras. No need to go slowly anymore, she sped through to the same timestamp.

Jordan's mother, turning to leave the pantry.

Nah, sarge, it's alright. Her mum was away—

"Oh fuck," she said, pushing the chair back fast enough for it to fall over. Kenny spun, running out of the room. She hurtled down the stairs, her feet thudding on them despite the carpet.

In the kitchen, Potter was cutting onions. Sandeman was stirring a huge pot. Both looked up as she entered.

"We've got a problem," she said. "Sandeman, get the weapons."

Like the pro she was, Sandeman dropped the wooden spoon into the chilli and immediately went through the side door to the garage. Locked from the outside, they'd judged it to be a secure enough place for most of their weapons.

"What's going on, sarge?" Potter still held the knife.

"Not sure. Ploughman was on camera, but Alex said she was away. The cameras show her right there, in the house."

"Shit," he said.

Sandeman kicked open the door, carrying three SA80s. She'd also stuffed a Glock into her belt. Potter went to her.

Kenny started to relax. This was going to be okay. Her team would rescue this situation, whatever it was. If Ploughman had found their cameras, found a way to fake the feed, then she'd just signed her own death warrant. Kenny grinned. Knowles would be happy they'd stopped a problem. Maybe she should contact him now, get clearance before she sanctioned killing the Ploughmans.

Nah. Knowles wouldn't check with anyone – he'd just act and deal with the consequences later.

She heard a gurgling sound, then a thud of metal on tiles and looked up but couldn't process what she was seeing. Sandeman slid down the wall, her throat open from ear to ear, with blood pouring out as she grabbed at her neck trying to hold the wound shut.

Potter aimed the Glock at Kenny.

"Sorry, sarge," he said and shot her between the eyes.

2

Jordan opened the door and retreated into the kitchen. Alex frowned, wondering where his welcome kiss (and more, oh God, so much more) was, but then he saw the other person in the kitchen.

"Alex, this is my mother, Emilia."

She didn't wear an expression of welcome and didn't look any happier as he proffered a hand to shake. Emilia took it after a beat, but the handshake lacked warmth. She didn't even bother to smile, let alone give it the chance to reach her eyes.

"Pleased to meet you." The lie died on his lips, becoming inaudible before he reached 'you'.

Emilia moved first, surging forward and grabbing Alex by the throat. Her fingers dug deep around his windpipe, shutting off his air. Eyes bulging, Alex gasped and clawed at her hand. *This is nuts. How strong is she?*

All the intelligence they had on the Ploughmans. The hours they'd spent watching. *What the hell was this?* Their intel was clearly missing something vital as he wasn't grappling with a *human* arm. Claws dug into his flesh, drawing spots of blood even as flashes of darkness appeared at the edge of his vision.

"Mum."

Darkness spread.

More urgently: "*Mum!*"

Emilia snarled at Jordan, but she acquiesced and released Alex. He sank to his knees, coughing and gasping for air, holding his throat. Blood seeped around his fingers, but it was already slowing: she hadn't done too much damage.

"What.... What..." More coughing. "Jesus, what the hell?"

Emilia knelt so she could be eye to eye. "We know exactly who you are."

Alex blinked away tears. "I don't—"

"Save it. Don't bother with your lies. We *know*."

He couldn't help it. Alex looked up at the light fitting hiding their camera and mic. Emilia caught the look and laughed. Alex quickly looked away, seeking Jordan but she was behind him. Surely she'd help?

"No-one is coming." Emilia slapped his head, making him look at her again, then she grabbed Alex's chin and forced his head up. "Get your thick squaddie head around that. Up you get."

Still nothing from Jordan. Through the pain shooting through his neck and the heaving he was still doing to get air into his lungs, that hurt the most.

Emilia dragged him to his feet, then pushed him back, forcing him to sit on a chair scraped from under the table. The scent of Jordan's perfume came to him as he felt a hand on his shoulder. *There she is.*

"You think you're all that, don't you? Keeping us here. Keeping us captive in suburbia." Emilia's voice was almost devoid of emotion, but

Alex felt the venom in the words, nonetheless. "You wanted us to be happy with our lot. So happy to be alive, we'd settle for this mundane shit for the rest of our miserable lives."

Alex looked between Jordan and Emilia, but both regarded him with contempt.

"Did you enjoy spying on me?" Jordan's voice, but unrecognisable. She sounded different to the breathless, eager woman he'd been sleeping with for the last few weeks. Her voice had changed, become harsher. Utterly devoid of anything except hatred. *What the fuck?*

"I didn't spy on you," he protested, but it sounded weak even to his ears.

"Yeah, right." Emilia beckoned her daughter like she might summon a waiter. Jordan went to her, standing to one side, a gap between her mother and her. She scowled at him; face twisted in an anger he hadn't thought her capable of even five minutes before.

"I really liked you."

"Yeah right."

"Show him," Emilia said.

"Follow me," Jordan said, turning away from him and heading into the house.

Alex wasn't sure his legs would hold him. They trembled underneath him, like he no longer had control over them, and he felt sick at the thought they would betray him now. He took a tentative step forward, and then he followed Jordan deeper into the house. He waited for her mother to follow, but she didn't.

Jordan opened the door that led down to the cellar-come-pantry and grinned at him. For a second, as her mask slipped, he saw the beautiful woman he'd fallen so hard for. The woman who had played him like a violin.

"I designed this."

He frowned. *Designed what?* He followed her downstairs, the nausea in his stomach not abating one iota. He knew this room from the cameras. Every morning, like clockwork, Emilia arriving to collect something from the—

Oh.

On their cameras, the room was a decent size, but small compared to the other rooms in the house. All four walls had expensive shelves – ridiculous really, who needs posh shelves to store food on? – all filled to the brim with food. One contained a decent wine rack, loaded no doubt with expensive wines.

Only now, one of the walls was gone. In its place, the opening to a tunnel stretching deep underground. Supports contained the walls at even spaces along its length, and halogen lamps highlighted the way through. She headed down the tunnel and he followed like a dutiful puppy, the irony not lost on him.

"You found our cameras then."

"Months ago. It was hard to play along, hard not to give the game up."

"You did this."

She nodded. "It was nice to use my expertise."

"Where does it go?"

"You know where."

He shook his head. "I really don't. Are you going to kill me?"

Her turn for a shake of the head. "Emilia has something she needs you for."

Alex hated himself, but relief flooded through him anyway. *Live for another day.*

"Do you really not know what's through here?"

"No," he said.

"The Original. His bones. Your lot buried them years ago."

He tried not to let the surprise show on his face, but knew he'd failed. The files had told him the whole story when he was first assigned here. Some random fell onto a bone in a cave and that's how this whole thing with the wolves started. He was a god or something.

After the final attack on Huntleigh, Knowles buried the bones deep in the cave where they'd been discovered. According to reports, top brass were upset he hadn't spoken to them first, and other top folk were upset he hadn't just ground them to dust. Knowles' defence had been the bones would reform.

Imagine that. Healing properties so great not even death could stop them.

"The bones," Alex said, earning a nod from Jordan. "You're heading for the bones."

"My mother has been looking for them for years. She thought she's found some in Germany years ago, but it was all bollocks. A hoax to try and unite the clans. Your lot persuaded us Jack Stadler—" *ah that was the random's name* "—was dead. Our only course of action was to get the bones back."

Jordan smiled again, brushing her hair away from her face. "We didn't have to dig too far to find the tunnels under the woods. Not long now until we have the bones."

"You haven't found them?" More relief. Alex could remember more of the report now. A soldier named Bryant had deliberately used the bones to infect himself, but it had sent him mad. That one act had killed so many people.

"Oh, we've found them alright. We just have a minor problem."

She continued along the tunnel, and he realised it was opening up, the lights not quite filling the space anymore. Before long, they were in a cave, with the roof high above them. Rocks made a natural barrier straight ahead, an enormous pile where the ceiling had collapsed at some point. To his left, the tunnel continued into darkness. No lights there.

"We think the bones are through there."

Alex shivered. The bones at the centre of so much death. "Why haven't you got them?"

"Watch." She threw a small rock into the tunnel and aimed a torch he hadn't realised she was carrying into the darkness.

At first, he couldn't see anything but darkness the torch failed to light. The darkness moved, seemed to vary in pitch and hue. *What the fuck? Don't go nuts now.* His eyes adjusted to the changing light and he could see things moving in the tunnel and he realised what he was looking at.

Spiders.

Hundreds of them, if not thousands. All clambering over each other, but not coming closer to the source of the light. He went cold, extremities tingling. Every fibre of his being screamed for him to run, flee, sprint away from the horrendous forms in the tunnel. Had the report mentioned spiders? He had a horrible, sinking feeling that one of Knowles' team had died because of spiders. Was this them? Surely not? How long did spiders live anyway?

"Stadler found a way through the spiders," Jordan said, switching the torch off and turning back to him. "They didn't attack him. His boy will lead us through."

Alex didn't respond to that. Jordan was clearly a whole new level of crazy and he just hadn't realised. How had she kept it from him? How hadn't he seen the warning signs? How come no-one else on the team had either?

"Are you serious? Stadler thinks it's a curse." He didn't know whether to feel grateful for the darkness hiding the horrific spiders or not. Already he could picture one scuttling towards them on its long thick legs. It running up his leg, maybe slipping inside his jeans first, crawling up his shin, it's light touch mixing horror with a tickle. Alex took a deep breath, trying to calm his breathing down.

It didn't work.

Jordan shrugged and made a face, her lips pursed. Then she turned on a heel and strode back the way she'd come.

"Why are you showing me this?"

"You need to know how desperate your situation is. You need to know we have thought of everything. Then you'll help us."

"Your mum is a fucking psycho. I'm not helping her."

"Your choice," she said. "But she will kill you."

Alex swallowed hard, his mouth and throat dry. He blinked rapidly at her. *Did I really not see any of this? Led by my dick again.* They were already back in the larder.

"My team will—"

"Your team is dead." She headed back up the stairs, not waiting to see if he would follow. He thought about running into the tunnel, making a break for it, but she turned the lights off, plunging them into a darkness that was almost absolute.

Alex had a horrific flash to the spiders surging down the tunnel, seeking his warm, moist places. He shivered, running after her.

"Did I mean nothing to you?"

Jordan watched him for a few moments, mulling her words over. "A fuck is a fuck."

3

They were back in the kitchen. Emilia was drinking tea, just like it was any other day in the Ploughman household. Alex felt sick at the normality of it all.

She grinned at them when they entered the kitchen. "What do you think?"

It took Alex a moment to realise she was talking to him. "You want to use a kid to walk through a nest of poisonous spiders, so you resurrect an ancient thing that killed loads of people. That about right?"

Emilia chuckled. "Yes."

"You're fucking mental."

"Watch your tongue, young man. You aren't that useful." Emilia spat her words, spittle flying from her lips.

"I'm not helping you."

"Oh, you will," Emilia said. "It's amazing what people will do to save their own skin."

Alex heart hammered in his chest, his blood rushing to his head. He knew the truth in her words. He didn't want to die today, nor tomorrow either if he could help it.

"What do you want from me?"

"It's simple, young man. Really simple. We need you to get on your little radio thing and tell everyone it's all okay down here."

Alex laughed, almost becoming hysterical. "You think that'll do it? You're fucked. I can't do it alone. It takes two to confirm any message we send."

Emilia grinned and pointed at the door. "Luckily, we already know that."

Alex swivelled in the chair, just in time to see someone enter the house. Someone with a big grin on his face. Someone who had spent far too much time in the pub with the locals.

Potter.

Fuck.

CHAPTER 11

1

"Got them?" Knowles turned to Towner. The younger man nodded and pressed a few buttons on the radio. It was part of the helicopter stash: portable radio, provisions and a lot of weapons and ammunition. They were still in the field next to the train, and had set up the radio at the top of the field, away from the helicopter and the train. People milled about: SOCOs covering the train tracks, next to which bodies were being laid out in a line; forensics on the train itself, doing whatever the hell they did at a time like this and uniforms watching the cordon around the scene. It would not be long before the press showed up en-masse.

And then the fun really begins. Knowles rubbed his head, then smoothed his hair down and tuned into Towner's conversation.

"How you doing, Alex?" Towner said, his face creasing into a large grin. "Still pining after that hot chick?"

"Do one Towner, you—."

"Nice one, Alex, especially as Captain Knowles is here and wants a word." Towner's smile didn't fade, even though the corners of his mouth twitched.

Knowles didn't say anything about the banter. There really wasn't a point, even though Alex had actually sounded pissed off. *No, that wasn't it.* Knowles lent over Towner and pressed the 'to talk' switch.

"Thorne, this is Captain Knowles."

"Yes sir, uh, sorry for the chatter sir."

"I don't give a shit about that, Thorne."

"Yes sir." Silence on the other end of the line. Then: "Sir, you've called early. Is there something wrong?"

"You have possible multiple hostiles heading your way. Is Kenny there?"

"That's a negative sir. I have Potter with me. The others are out on errands at this time."

Towner glanced at Knowles; grin replaced with a furrowed brow. Knowles hadn't seen such a serious expression on the young man's face before.

"Get him on speaker, please."

They heard a click, then Potter's booming voice came over the air.

"Good afternoon, sir, always makes a day brighter to hear from you. To what do we owe the pleasure?"

Knowles chewed his lip. "Cut the crap, Potter. I know you're bored shitless down there, but just apply to rotate out next time."

"Yes sir." Even over the air, Knowles knew the man rolled his eyes. *Potter. He would need some serious dressing down next time they met.*

"You have three hostile wolves possibly heading your way with a hostage."

"Shit."

"That's awful!"

The swearing came from Potter, the tamer response from Thorne.

"The hostage is a child. A boy called Josh Stadler. He is not to be harmed under any circumstances. If you see these men, you are to exterminate them immediately, but not if there is any risk of harm to the boy. Understood?"

Both men confirmed, Thorne with a curt, "Affirmative, sir."

"Pictures of the men are coming your way, check your secure comms. Make no mistake gents, these men are dangerous. Get the others up to speed when they get back. You need to be vigilant."

"Any idea when they will come sir?"

"Hopefully not at all, Thorne, hopefully we'll intercept before they get anywhere near you, but it's best to be prepared."

"Absolutely sir."

"Knowles out."

He killed the connection but could see Towner still wore a troubled expression.

"Spill it Towner, what's up?"

"Alex was weird, sir."

"Thorne? Explain."

"I grew up with him, sir, South London and all that. I've never heard him speak so long without swearing. He used some, you know, sophisticated language too. All that 'affirmative' and 'negative' bollocks. It just didn't sound like him."

Knowles would have chuckled at the thought of those particular words being considered 'sophisticated language', but his heart sank at Towner's words.

"I think he may be in trouble, sir." Towner's face was pale, but he was finally looking at Knowles with a measure of respect. *No, not respect. Worry. He's worried.*

"How long have you known Alex Thorne?"

"We signed on together. I've known him since primary school."

"Shit."

"Yeah."

Miller ambled over, looking far too relaxed for the day they were having. "Something wrong?" he said as soon as he saw the expression on Towner's face. The cuts on his face glowed in the midday sun. A tablet dangled by his side.

"You sure about this?" Knowles asked, ignoring Miller.

"Pretty sure. That didn't sound like Thorney, you know? Maybe he was trying to give me a message."

"He did sound nervous."

"But Potter sounded okay." Towner shrugged, doubt creeping into his voice.

"Sir," Miller said. "You need to see this." He held the tablet up, showing a photo. Two men, sat in a car on a motorway. Shadows in the seats behind. Knowles recognised the men immediately.

"Where was that taken?"

"M5, sir, just above Birmingham."

Heading South. Not unexpected. "When?"

"Not sure. Around an hour ago."

"And we're only getting it now? For fuck's sake!" Knowles looked for something to hit, punch or kick but couldn't see anything that wouldn't break his hand or foot as a result. *Sitting here, babysitting Jack whilst those shitheads got further away.* He nodded at Miller. "Get the pilot ready. We're making another flight soon."

"Sir." Miller jogged over to the helicopter without another word. Knowles tapped Towner on the shoulder. "Get them back on the line. I want to know if there's a problem." A distant cough made him turn around.

Jack stood there, shielding his eyes from the bright light. Behind him, Penfold leant on the helicopter and watched carefully whilst eating from a tin. *At least she is vigilant.*

"Shit," Knowles muttered. "Get them on the line, Towner. I'm not sure how much longer he's going to be calm."

"We wouldn't like him when he's angry."

"Trust me, you won't. Do it now."

2

Alex switched the mic off and sat back. Potter clapped him on the shoulder and grinned.

"See, son, that wasn't so bad, was it?"

Alex clenched his teeth together and said nothing. It was weird being back in the house like this. A prisoner. The first thing he'd seen when they marched him back was Kenny's body. Then the others, laid out in a line, like they were at a kid's sleepover. His legs buckled at the sight, but Potter held him up, forcing him to look, saying, "Don't let this be you."

Don't let this be you.

Alex kept looking for a way out, but Potter was next to him all the time. He'd even gone to the toilet, and Potter had come with him. The big man's grin so firmly in place the whole time that Alex wanted to smash his teeth in.

He didn't have a clue what the Ploughmans would do with the bodies, and surely it wouldn't be that long before they began to stink. Alex had seen enough dead bodies to know they would soon leak fluids and swell. A matter of days, a week at most, until skin erupted as the organs inside decomposed and became mush. Eventually the bodies would have loose skin, then the teeth would fall out, but he guessed he'd be one of their ranks long before that happened.

Kenny's body had affected him the most, but his captors had all his team here. Sandeman. Wijnberg. Howell. All gone, in Devon of all places. He knew he had to get a warning to the Captain, but with Potter sat next to him, it would be difficult, if not impossible. Hearing Towner rip him gave him the idea to not respond as he would normally. The banter between them was never, ever clean.

Was it enough? Had he figured it out?

Alex had no way of knowing. Survival was his sole goal now. Live long enough for someone to rescue him.

Bollocks to that. First chance, I'm out of here.

"All good here?" Emilia said, entering the cramped comms room. All screens to the Ploughmans were off now, but the others still had active feeds.

"The kid was a champ." Potter rested his hand on Alex's shoulder.

"Good. My brothers are on their way. Change of plans," she shrugged. "Not a big deal, but it should be enough to clear a path."

Potter nodded, his lips a thin line that slowly turned to a smile. "I've proven my loyalty."

"Patience, patience. You can be first to the bones."

Alex's mouth was dry and his eye twitched. So Potter was not one of *them*, or at least not yet. His treachery came down to simple biology – he actually *wanted* to be one of those things.

"What if this change to the plan doesn't work like we wanted?"

Emilia's stare made Alex's blood run cold. Even Potter, with his size, took an involuntary step backwards.

"Do you think my brother has made an error?"

Potter shook his head so hard he looked like an overgrown toddler. "No, of course not."

"Good." Emilia's face returned to the sour expression she usually wore. *Resting bitch face.* "Now, lock him up."

Potter reached over to drag Alex to his feet.

The radio buzzed again.

3

"Thorne?" Knowles' voice, loud and clear over the radio.

Potter let Alex go then scrabbled for the microphone. "It's Potter, sir, Alex has just stepped out."

"Well get him back then."

"I, uh, I think he's gone for a shit, sir." Potter winced at his poor choice of words.

"I see Devon has done nothing to improve your manners."

"Sorry sir." Potter failed to keep the smirk out of his voice.

"When are you expecting the others back?"

"Not sure sir. Soon, I guess."

"I need Kenny to contact me as soon as she returns."

"Is there a problem sir?"

"No, no. Just some info I need to give to Kenny."

"Well, just tell me sir and I'll pass it on."

Silence from the other end. Potter's eyes flicked between Alex and Emilia. Everyone in the room held their breath. Alex was pale, or somehow, even more pale. He hadn't had colour in those cheeks since he'd seen the bodies of his former colleagues.

Potter made to open the communication lines again, but Emilia tapped his arm and shook her head. Then, after what seemed a year but was probably only a few seconds, the radio sparked into life again.

"It's confidential, Potter. You keep doing what you do and get Kenny to contact me when she is able. Clear?"

"Yes, sir."

"Excellent. Knowles out."

Potter put the mic back on the tabletop with a frown.

"Do we have a problem, Potter?"

He nodded. "Yeah, I think so. We have about an hour before he calls us back."

Alex started laughing. "You're so fucked."

Emilia stared at him, eyes wide and lip curled in the beginnings of a snarl. Earlier, Emilia's stare had made Alex's blood run cold, but now it made him laugh even harder. Something about extreme danger and the desire to laugh were intrinsically linked.

"Sorry." The apology did nothing to stop his giggling fit. He held up a hand and shook his head. "Sorry, okay?"

Emilia closed the distance between them in a heartbeat. Too fast for Alex to realise he'd made a fatal error. Her mouth and jaw stretched, becoming longer as she opened wide and bit Alex's face. The younger man screamed: a wet, gurgling noise abruptly ending when Emilia's teeth punctured first his jugular and then his windpipe. She pulled her head back, ripping Alex's jaw, nose and neck away from his body. He would not leave a handsome corpse behind. Blood spurted from the wounds, coating the carpet and walls, as he collapsed, already dead.

"Shit, Emilia."

She spun, advancing on Potter, who stepped back holding his hands up in a mirror of Alex from a moment ago. "Please, Emilia, no, please."

Her face returned to normal as she licked her lips, sighing with satisfaction. "Relax, Potter. I'm not going to kill you. Remember, you're one of us. Practically one of the family."

But I'm not. Potter couldn't help the thought, but he had the sense not to give it flight.

"That little shit had that coming for weeks." Emilia spat on Alex's corpse. "The way he treated my daughter, like she was a piece of meat. And they think *we're* the animals."

Yeah, but you asked her to sleep with him.

"We have an hour before Knowles thinks something is up. Another few hours until he gets here. We have a lot to do before then."

"I thought we were waiting for your brothers."

"We are. They're nearly here. Come on, we don't want to be late."

4

"We need that bird in the air now," Knowles roared as soon as the line went dead.

Jack had nearly reached him and Knowles could see his eyes were still red-rimmed and puffy. He seemed smaller somehow, not helped by Penfold walking a few paces behind him, still eating from a can.

"Sir, pilot says we have to make a fuel stop. We'll not reach Devon on what he's got left," Miller yelled from the helicopter.

Knowles swore. "Okay, okay, let's go. We've got to get to Huntleigh."

"I'm coming with you."

Knowles turned to Jack and shook his head. "No way. You're too emotional."

Jack nodded. "Yeah, yeah I am. But fuck that, Knowles, these men have my boy."

"We don't know they are there."

"That's where they're headed, you said so yourself."

His fucking hearing.

"Jack, please."

"Don't make me force you Knowles."

"Is that a threat, Jack?" Knowles squared his shoulders, jutted his chin out. A pointless gesture, but it made him feel better. "Not a good idea to threaten me."

Jack's shoulders sagged and Knowles thought more tears would come. None did, so perhaps he was finally all cried out. He held his hands up, placating. "Not threatening, Knowles. These men are dangerous. You could use me."

"Not to create a bloodbath."

"They. Have. My. Son," Jack said through gritted teeth.

And they killed your wife. Knowles ran a hand through his hair. "As soon as Josh is safe, you leave – clear?"

"Crystal."

"Don't make me regret this, Jack."

Knowles stomped away, a sick feeling in his stomach. *Here we go again.* At least this time, it was just three wolves. At least this time he knew what he was dealing with.

Miller came back. "Pilot says we need to stop to refuel, before heading to Devon, sir."

"Radio ahead, get the refuel ready. I don't want to waste time."

"Sir." Miller turned to go, but Knowles put a hand on his arm.

"Keep it on the quiet though, Miller, please. We don't want to start a panic."

Miller nodded and jogged back to the Wildcat.

"Wheels up in five," Knowles roared. "All gear loaded, weapons checked. Look lively, folks, we're going to fucking Devon."

Again.

Chapter 12

1

Harry sat next to the kid, who was less annoying as he was asleep. Harry, too, kept drifting off, but he would jerk awake, hitting his head on the window. Chris smirked every time this happened, enjoying the other man's discomfort.

Rich had also slept, but he jerked awake then sat bolt upright. The suddenness of the action would have scared Chris if he hadn't seen it so many times before. Rich was carrying the same trauma and shit from their childhood as Chris, not that Chris would ever use words like 'trauma'. Deep down, he knew their fondness for violence wasn't normal, but he enjoyed it too much to explore the reasons, or even the fact there might be a better approach to most situations than lashing out.

"Where are we?" Rich's voice was thick with sleep, and he shook his head, slapping his cheeks to try and wake himself more fully.

"A30, just about to turn off. Huntleigh is about twenty, maybe thirty minutes away." The miles had passed without incident. Chris had kept the car to eighty, reasoning they would stand out more if they went slower. He was pretty much done with this shit-heap of a car though.

"Have you told Emilia?"

Chris nodded. A burner phone, stolen from a posh service station near Gloucester, sat in a cradle clamped to the air-vent.

"You know they'll have seen us on CCTV by now, right?" Chris phrased his question carefully: he didn't want to antagonise his brother or make him think he was doubting his plan.

"Yeah, but fuck 'em." Rich rolled his head, stretching his neck. "Man, I'll be glad to see the back of this shitmobile. By the time those soldiers get here, we'll be through the tunnel. As soon as we have the bones, they won't be able to stop us."

Chris grinned. They were really going to do this. Something they'd talked about for years but never managed to actually do. Emilia had kept in touch through burner phones and dummy websites (when they'd had access to laptops or smartphones). Each update had been about the progress of the tunnel through to the burial chamber under Huntleigh woods. *Original bones. The power to make anyone an Original. Fucking A.*

They'd hit a snag with the spiders. Emilia was bitten as soon as she set foot in the tunnel, and it was only because Jordan dragged her away that she survived. If she'd been human, the poison would have killed her.

Chris shuddered. *Why did it have to be spiders?*

"It'll be good to see Emilia."

"Yeah," Rich said. "Been too long."

Conversation over. Chris swallowed and tapped the steering wheel without rhythm.

"That's really fucking irritating," Rich said, and Chris stopped immediately. They really had been in the car far too fucking long.

2

Dartmoor receded in the rear-view mirror as they turned off the A30 and headed north. Here, fields broke the monotony of motorways and dual carriageways, stretching for miles in all directions. An occasional wind turbine broke the line between field and sky. A tractor pulled out in front of them, making them slow to an unbearable pace, and Chris thought about forcing the driver off the road. He pictured ripping his throat out, opening his stomach to get at the good stuff, the meat being tastier with the community service he'd be doing.

He chuckled to himself, earning another baleful stare from his brother.

"Christ, my neck," Harry said from the rear seat. He yawned, trying to stretch, but there wasn't any room in the car, and he only made himself more uncomfortable.

"Are we nearly there yet?" Josh was awake too. Chris ground his teeth. *Are we there yet?* Jesus Christ. Again, more memories came to mind. His father losing his shit on long journeys when they were kids. Yelling at all three kids, yelling at their mother. It was years before Chris realised the shouts were backed up with fists as soon as the children were in bed. Rich ripping his throat out was the best thing that ever happened to their family.

"Not far," Harry said. "Relax, kid, this'll soon be over."

"I want my mum and dad."

"They're not here. They won't ever be here. They're gone." Rich said, spitting the words, proving that parental skills were nurtured rather than natural.

Josh's bottom lip slid out, and tears welled in his eyes. They rolled down his cheeks, and he sobbed. Harry put his arm around the kid's shoulders and hugged him close, actually shushing him and making reassuring noises.

"What the fuck are you doing Harry?" Chris said, meeting his eyes in the mirror.

"This doesn't need to be worse than it already is. He's a kid."

Rich laughed. "You're such a soft touch Harry. A proper fucking pansy. Why the hell did we follow you for so long?"

"You didn't follow me, you—"

"Do you know what a rhetorical question is?" Rich turned, resting an arm on the back of his seat. Thick cords of muscle stood out.

Chris felt relief that someone else was here to take his brother's anger. If that made *him* weak and pathetic, so be it. Someone else was always weaker and more pathetic.

Harry was wise enough to keep his mouth shut. Rich held his gaze for far too long, before nodding, grinning and turning to face the front.

"Overtake this farmer dick, Chris, or so help me, I'll fuck the driver up and then you."

3

Jordan ran outside as soon as the car crunched onto the drive. She pulled open the gate and rushed forwards, jumping on Rich as he climbed out of the car.

"Hey, unky Rich," she said, climbing off him. He grinned at her – the first genuine grin Harry had ever seen – and stretched.

"Nice to see you too, baby girl."

"Hey Jordan," Chris said, slamming his own door shut. "How's tricks?"

Her smile faltered just for a moment, but she recovered it before Chris noticed. "Hi Chris."

Harry watched the exchange without comment but storing information anyway. *Why does she prefer Rich to Chris? Shit, why did she like either of them?*

"Who's this?" Jordan made a play of looking Harry up and down with a sly smile on her face.

"I'm Harry."

"He's Harry," Chris said. "Someone we picked up in London."

Harry bristled at the comment but took a deep breath in lieu of saying anything. "My wife found them, and we all went to what we thought was a safe house."

"Your wife?" Jordan couldn't hide the disappointment in her voice.

"It weren't that safe though, were it?" Chris said with a scowl. "Been chased halfway across the country by soldiers, ain't we?"

"Well, you'll soon be safe all the time."

Harry turned to see a woman who looked like a smaller, feminine version of Rich, down to the same beady, mean eyes and hard face. She was the same size as Harry though, which made her a good few inches shorter than her brothers. The three smiled at each other, and then Chris pulled her into a hug with a big laugh.

"Where's the boy?" Emilia said, when Chris finally released her from the hug.

"In the car," Harry said, and Jordan peered into the vehicle.

"He's so cute!"

"Jordan." Emilia's voice was soft, but the edge to it shut her up immediately. She closed the car door, leaving the kid inside. "You sure it's him?"

Rich nodded. "Definitely. Took him from his mum myself."

"And his father?"

A shrug. "No idea. Back in Scotland, moping about his dead wife probably."

"Are you sure?" Emilia frowned. "Dead wife?"

Another nod from Rich. "Ripped her throat out. Would've done the same to him if I'd had the chance."

Harry pulled Josh into him more, almost crushing him against his waist. With his hand, he covered Josh's ear.

"I doubt it," Emilia said.

Rich's smile vanished. "I don't lie."

Emilia took a step back. She couldn't help it. Even after all this time, her brother's stare made her blood run cold. "I didn't mean that."

"No? What did you mean? Do you think I wouldn't be able to kill him?"

Emilia shook her head. "If he's an Original then it would have been a tough fight—"

"There's no buts here," Rich said, and Chris sniggered.

"Originals can heal," Emilia said.

"Original my arse." Rich headed down the drive, towards the house. "He was no Original."

"But the bones?"

"Something else, maybe, I don't know. He was far too much of a wuss to be an almighty Original." Rich looked back at them. "I'm hungry. You got some food, sis?"

4

They ate chicken pasta with a creamy spinach sauce. Emilia barely said two words during the entire meal; Jordan didn't keep her mouth shut. Rich smiled at her with a paternal grace, Chris with something unwholesome. Emilia beamed with pride as Jordan relayed information about her university days and how she had worked out the maths needed for the tunnel underneath Huntleigh Woods.

Harry watched and ate, ate and watched. *This has to be the most fucked up family dynamic I've ever seen.* The way Chris watched Jordan, his eyes darting back to her face every few seconds, as if they had wandered somewhere else – somewhere more interesting perhaps. The thought made Harry nauseous.

Rich and Emilia though, that was a whole other dynamic, no less fucked up, but not as pervy. They would both burst at the seams if they were any more proud. Harry continued to eat the food, watching and learning. *There are weaknesses here.* Weaknesses that could be exploited to give Josh a fighting chance of getting out of this alive. *Surely they won't kill a kid?* He wished he could be certain of that.

"What happens now?" Harry put his fork down and pushed the empty plate away.

Rich and Emilia exchanged a glance, then Rich gave an 'after you' gesture to her.

Rich stood, wooden chair legs scraping on stone tiles. "Time to see this tunnel of yours."

"No," Josh said.

Rich looked at him, taking in his thin lips and set jaw. His fists were balled up tight by his sides. "No?"

"I'm not going with you. I want to go home."

Chris slapped him hard enough to knock the boy to his knees. He looked up at Chris, tears in his eyes, hand to his already red cheek. "You'll do what I fucking say, you little shit."

Harry stood in front of Josh, hand on Chris's chest. "Take it easy, man. He's just a kid."

"Not cool, Uncle Chris." Jordan knelt next to Josh and wiped his tears away. "Don't cry, little man, Chris won't hurt you anymore, I promise." She glared at her uncle.

Rich dragged his brother back away from the boy. "Leave him alone. We need him."

"We don't need a *kid*."

Rich shrugged. "Emilia thinks we do and that's good enough for me. Look, we didn't drag him across the country to not even try this."

Harry thought it was the most reasonable Rich had ever sounded. Emilia's effect?

"It'll work." Emilia was already at the door to the kitchen. "Stadler fell onto the bones and became the Original. We can do the same."

"Stadler's no Original." Chris said. "Weren't you listening?"

"The stories say otherwise." As soon as the words were out, she held up a placating hand. "I know what you think you saw, but I think there's some truth to those rumours."

Chris laughed again. "This is madness."

"You believed enough to bring *him* here." Emilia opened the door and head through, shouting, "Come on!" as she went.

Rich followed immediately, with Chris in tow. Jordan helped Josh to his feet, but he kept his eyes on Harry.

"My dad will come and save me."

Harry met Jordan's eyes, seeing a mirror of his own fear there. *I hope not kid, I hope not, for his sake.* Out loud, he said, "Come on, let's get this over with."

5

The tunnel in the pantry felt cooler than the kitchen. Emilia led the way, followed closely by Rich and Chris. Jordan and Josh came next, just in front of Harry, with the young woman holding Josh's hand. Behind him, a tall, burly man – introduced as Potter – made sure Harry kept up.

Straight off the bat, Harry had an instant dislike to Potter. He smelt wrong for a start. *Human.* He couldn't work out why a human was helping the wolves. Hell, he couldn't work out why the wolves were putting up with the human.

They trudged along the tunnel, sometimes being forced into single file where it narrowed but it would soon widen again. Josh kept looking back at Harry, those big eyes searching for something Harry couldn't give him. Before long, they emerged into a bigger, open cave with another tunnel opposite heading deeper underground.

A slight breeze blew through, so slight as to be negligible. Nothing in the cave moved. Electric lanterns, strung up around the perimeter, illuminated the empty cavern. Cables ran back to the house, neatly bracketed to the ground up against the tunnel wall. It took Harry a moment to realise just how empty the cavern was. No cobwebs, no small bugs, nothing you might expect to see underground. He shuddered.

This place felt *wrong.*

"The Original's bones are through there?" Rich pointed at the tunnel, moving towards the opening.

Emilia nodded. "With the spiders."

"You think this is where Jack Stadler fell all those years ago? You think the bones of an Original are in *there*?" Sarcasm and doubt dripped from his words.

"I don't think, I know." Emilia nodded at Potter. "Tell him. Tell him what you saw."

"This is where Jack Stadler fell. It's right through there. He landed on a bone; it went right through him." Potter mimed a bone coming out of his chest.

"How do you know this?" Rich said.

"I've read the files, seen stuff with my own eyes." He pointed at the tunnel. "Down there is the holy grail for your kind."

Emilia pulled Rich back from the entrance. "Don't be stupid, Richard. This is no myth and is no place for your hard man act."

Act? Harry was pretty sure there was no acting with Rich. He really was nuts.

"Look, it's simple," Emilia said. "Stadler fell into a cave. Enough people believed Stadler to be an Original to storm an army base."

"I was one of them," Harry muttered.

"Potter read all about it, and has friends who were part of the clean-up crew. The army sealed this cave for a reason. They have posted soldiers in the woods for a reason." She paused, pushing her chin out, then pointed into the darkness. "The reason is at the end of that tunnel."

"I still say it's bullshit."

"So why have you come all this way?" Emilia grinned at him, but there was no humour or warmth in the look. "To play happy families with your sister and niece?"

Rich balled a fist, but didn't throw the punch, despite the rage clear on his face. Emilia continued talking, oblivious to, or uncaring of the danger she was putting herself in. "Look, it is true. All of it. I swear to you once we have those bones, we can be a force again. We can live together again without fear of the soldiers kicking our door in."

"You took care of the soldiers here without a problem."

"We had help." She nodded at Potter. "Also, Jordan distracted one of them."

"You slept with a human soldier?" Chris's mouth dropped open. Harry could see his brain struggling with the twin images of Jordan naked, and her fucking a human. That nausea returned.

Jordan's smile fell. "I did what was necessary. Get that look off your face. We'd be crawling with soldiers if it weren't for me."

Emilia pulled her into another hug, proud of her daughter.

Jesus. Harry couldn't wrap his head being proud of someone using sex to manipulate a situation. Maybe he was a prude, but it just didn't seem right. *One step away from prostitution.* The fact she seemed to have enjoyed it also sat uneasy with him.

"Enough," Emilia said. She picked a torch up from a small pile of them on the floor of the cave. "Look."

She aimed the beam down the tunnel, but it's meagre light failed to illuminate much.

"What am I looking at?" Rich was typically gruff.

"Just wait."

Something moved at the edge of the light, but it had gone by the time Emilia aimed the beam that way. Movement always seemed just out of view. Rich frowned, squinting into the darkness.

"What is that?" Chris whispered, moving to get a better view.

"Spiders," Emilia said and then the tunnel was full of them, all climbing over each other and moving towards the tunnel mouth. Thick legs scratched on stone and against other legs, creating a horrible *skittering* sound.

Without meaning to, Rich and Chris both took a step back.

"Relax," Emilia said. "They don't come any further forward than there." She pointed at the opening to the cave. "We're perfectly safe here."

"They're enormous," Harry said. "What the hell? Spiders don't grow that big in the UK."

"Someone forgot to tell them." Chris's braying laugh again. Harry so wanted to smash his face in.

"I tried to go in there," Emilia said, pale in the torchlight. "Jordan got me out. I was in bed for a week."

"Pussy," Chris said.

"Shut the fuck up Chris." This came from Jordan. The venom in her words was audible. "She nearly died."

Rich glanced at Emilia; the question writ large on his face. She nodded. "It was close," she said. "Thank god Jordan was home that weekend."

"You got bit?" A nod. "How many times?"

Emilia looked away, embarrassed to answer. "One."

"Shit."

"Yeah. We can't get in there." Emilia turned to Josh. "But he can."

"Wait, what?" Harry said.

"He can make it through there because he's human."

"So's he." Harry jabbed a finger at Potter.

Emilia shook her head. "The only person we know who survived the spiders is Stadler. His father." She nodded at Josh. "He was born after Stadler became an Original. He'll survive."

"No, that's not right," Harry said. "Stadler was an Original the day Josh was born. You've got this wrong."

"And how the fuck do you know that?" Rich's face contorted with anger.

Harry swallowed. How could he explain? He used to run in a pack, led by a guy called Callum, someone who made Rich seem like a reasonable and calm bloke. Callum had said the boy was born following an accident to his dad. Had the information first hand from a bloke called Steve who knew Stadler.

"Look, I know, okay. Whatever happened to Stadler, it has nothing to do with his son."

"They share genes, dickhead."

"Rich, you send this boy into that tunnel, he will die."

Josh gazed at Harry, his bottom lip quivering. "I don't want to die."

Rich grabbed Harry by the shirt. "Someone is going down there, so it may as well be the kid." He pushed Harry into the wall behind which he hit hard enough to force the air out of his lungs. He watched in slow motion, trying to breathe, as Rich pulled Josh towards the tunnel.

"Wait," Harry gasped. "Burn them. Burn the spiders first, then send him."

"We burnt them last time," Emilia said, lip curling into a sneer. "Potter got us some incendiary grenades. It cleared the path, but only for a time. They came back almost immediately."

Harry wracked his brain, trying to remember everything he could about grenades. As a kid, he'd been obsessed with military history, and some of that remained in his memory. "They burn hot and fast, correct?" He wanted Potter to nod, grin, do something to acknowledge him and for a long moment, it was as if he hadn't spoken at all.

And then the big man nodded. "Yeah, that's right."

"Okay then, so maybe something that burns longer will help."

Rich scowled, feeling his grip on the situation slipping. "Why the fuck do you care about this kid?"

"Who said I care?" Harry saw Josh flinch at the words and hated himself. A few days ago he really wouldn't have cared, but he kept seeing Flo's face. Her kindness. Her empathy. She would not have stood by and let this kid be sacrificed, no matter the end game. "Look, if he can do this, then there's no problem, but what if we're wrong?" Emphasis on the word 'we're'. "We send him through the spiders, and he dies before he gets anywhere near the bones. How does that help anyone? Let's get some alcohol, burn the shit out of them."

Rich's expression turned into a grin so demonic Harry wished he could see the scowl again. "Now you're talking."

6

It took less than fifteen minute to raid the alcohol cupboard. Emilia looked pained at some of the more expensive whiskeys being taken, but both Rich and Chris were ecstatic. Rich, in particular, looked like a kid at Christmas.

They stuffed the tops with rags then travelled back to the cave. Harry and Josh had stayed there with Potter, sitting in a silence only periodically broken by Josh repeating, "I want to go home."

The others laid out their improvised weapons, then stood back, surveying them. Chris collected a couple, shaking them to make sure the rags were well coated in alcohol.

"Stand back," he said with a grin, producing a lighter from his pocket.

"Well back," Potter said. "I've seen these go badly wrong and explode in people's hands. Back into the tunnel." He led them a short distance down the tunnel.

"We should let Josh go," Harry said, grabbing Rich's arm. "They'll kill us all to get at him."

Rich gave a pointed look at Harry's hand until he let go. "Who, Harry? Who'll kill us to get him? His parents are dead."

"Fire in the hole!" Chris ran towards them, giggling. "I always wanted to say that."

Behind him, the tunnel brightened as air whooshed past them. Harry, Rich and Chris returned to the cavern, not sure what they were seeing.

Every spider around the mouth of the cave burned with an intense orange flame, but they didn't move; didn't scuttle away. It was like they stayed there, staring at the men as they burned. Some of the spiders popped, earning fresh giggles from Chris and filling the air with a strange acrid smell that burnt the back of Harry's throat.

"Done?" Emilia came up behind them as the flames died down. The slight breeze sent the smoke away, deeper into the tunnels. Small pockets of the spiders were still on fire and further down the tunnel, as the smoke cleared, they could see more spiders waiting.

"These guys are hardcore," Chris said. They all coughed as the smoke cleared.

"There's still some left," Rich said. "Hit them again."

Chris picked up another bottle, lit it and hurled it into the tunnel. It shattered on one of the walls, and flames leapt up it, catching hundreds of spiders in their wake. Still they didn't move. Still they sat, watching as they died.

"This is pretty fucked up," Chris said. He'd stopped giggling.

"Yeah," Rich said. His scowl hadn't changed. "Again."

Chris threw two more bottles into the tunnel as Harry dragged Josh back into the cavern. They waited for the flames to die down and the smoke to clear. The breeze, feeling stronger now, cleared the air once more.

"Where's the smoke going?" Harry peered along the length of the tunnel, but the light fell away beyond the edge of the fire.

"Tunnels," Emilia said. "Could be going anywhere. Only needs a tiny crack for air to get through."

Rich knelt down in front of Josh and handed him a torch. "Go down the tunnel. You're looking for some bones. Any bones."

"Run if you see spiders," Harry said.

"No," Josh said, jutting his chin out. "I'm not doing it."

Rich slapped him so hard his feet left ground. Josh hit the deck with a thump and scrambled backwards away from him, eyes wide. Tears welled in his eyes, but he didn't cry out.

Rich went to take a step forward, but Harry stood in front of him and put a hand on his chest. He could feel the muscle straining there, and his legs went cold. Rich turned an impassive face towards him.

"Get the fuck out of the way."

"No." Harry was surprised his voice didn't break or waver at all. "He won't do it if you hit him again, for fuck's sake."

"Worked on me," Rich said, but he didn't take another step.

"Look, the bones will be heavy, he might not be able to lift them."

"We don't even know if they'll be there." Rich's voice was quiet, and Harry had to strain to hear him. The undercurrent of menace, however, was loud and clear.

"They're there," Emilia said. "The spiders are proof there's something unnatural down here."

"Not really," Chris said. "They're just fucking spiders."

"I'll go with him," Potter said. He picked up one of the two remaining bottles.

"Why you?" Chris peeled himself off the wall, squaring up to the man.

Potter matched him, eye to eye, reminding Harry of just how big both men were. "You can't go down there, remember? The spiders nearly did for your sister. If they're not going to attack the little man, they might not attack me."

"Might," Harry said. "You don't know that for sure."

Potter shrugged. "We need the bones, yes?"

"If they're real," Rich said, drawing another impatient sigh from Emilia.

Potter smiled at Emilia. "Let me do this for you. Show you I'm with you once and for all."

She returned the smile and nodded. Potter dragged Josh to his feet, pulling his hand away from his face. He inspected the red mark and nodded.

"No lasting damage, little man. It hurt, right?"

Josh glared at him, face full of impotent rage.

Potter gazed at him for a moment, and Harry thought Josh might get hit again, but then the big man threw back his head and howled with laughter. "Good spirit, kid, that's going to help."

He pushed Josh into the tunnel entrance, and then followed, feet crunching with each step.

7

The light from their torches faded quickly as they disappeared into the tunnel. Harry found he was holding his breath and let it out slowly.

"You getting attached to that kid, Harry?" Rich's eyes were cold.

"I don't want anyone to die who doesn't have to," Harry said.

"You've changed your tune."

"Not really. I was angry about Flo, but she wouldn't want *this*. Wouldn't want the boy killed because of us."

"We're hunters," Rich said.

"Yeah, damn straight." Chris nodded, moving so he was at right angles to Harry.

"Maybe so, but not kids, man. Anything but kids."

"What if the kid has a gun?" Chris said. His expression said *Gotcha*.

"He doesn't." Harry shrugged. Chris was a fuckwit at times, but now he was reaching a new low.

"He'll grow up to have one," Rich said.

"Maybe. Maybe not." Harry ran a hand through his hair. "We should let him go."

"Are you nuts?" Rich jabbed a finger into his chest. "He's our bargaining chip for when the soldiers get here. Unless these bones are real, in which case we won't need him."

"So we're all going to become Originals? Is that it? What happens to Josh then?"

Rich smiled. "If we're all Originals, it won't fucking matter, will it?"

"What do you mean?"

"Let them send an army. If we're all Originals, we'll kill them all."

CHAPTER 13

1

The journey had taken a long time, and Knowles was trying not to let his frustration show. Jack sat next to him, eyes closed, but he wasn't sleeping. His leg jittered up and down like it had a mind of its own, and his hand had a tremor that didn't look like Jack was staying calm. *Just another thing to worry about.*

Miller, Towner and Penfold were all chatting and joking, letting off steam. He let them. No sense in stopping them have some fun whilst travelling. It helped ease the stress and hell, it wasn't *that* long ago that he would have been with them. Bailey was asleep, with his head resting against the helicopter door. How he could sleep through the noise was beyond Knowles, especially as he hadn't been in one for at least five years. Probably longer. *Shit. I am getting too old for this.*

"Two minutes out," the pilot said. Knowles nodded and held two fingers up to the team. He nudged Bailey, having to repeat the action twice to wake the man. Bailey rubbed his eyes, yawning and trying to stretch in the confined space.

"First stop is the safe house," Knowles said. "Get the lie of the land from them. Be alert. We don't really know what we're walking into."

"It might be fine," Bailey said.

Knowles gave him a withering look.

The engines changed pitched, and Knowles' stomach leapt into his mouth as they descended at speed, landing with a thump. Miller had the door open, and they all disembarked within seconds. Jack was last, stepping cautiously into the field.

Thick hedges bordered the field, and a slope rolled away down to dense wood behind them. Glorious golden sunlight highlighted the sheer variety of greens they could all see. Ahead of them, beyond the hedges, they could see the top floor and roofs of a row of houses.

Jack took a deep breath full of familiar smells. The grass. The trees. The sheep in the next field over. He had a brief recollection of eating one of those many years ago, but he had neither a clear memory of it, nor was there any chance they'd be the same sheep. He remembered the last time he came here with Knowles, coming out of a similar helicopter. That time, it'd been to save both his wife and son. Now it was just –

Thoughts of Katie hit him like a sledgehammer. Her smile. Her scent. Her ability to swear like a sailor or a character in a Tarantino movie. Her kindness. Her devotion to him and Josh.

Grief threatened to overwhelm him again, and he tried to bury the thoughts. His focus had to be rescuing Josh. *Don't forget killing the bastards that did all this, Jack.* The Wolf, still so close to the surface, still looking for a way to be let off the leash. *You need me. You need me for what comes next. You know it, Jack.* Jack shook his head, trying to clear it, earning a concerned look from Knowles.

"You okay?" Knowles said.

Jack tried to smile but ended up just nodding at the other man. There would be plenty of time to grieve once he knew Josh was safe.

Plenty of time to help his son through this. Plenty of time to deal with rage.

"This way," Knowles said. He led them across the field and out onto a road. The soldiers all seemed to know where they were going, except for Bailey, who stayed at Jack's side.

"Where's your safe house?" Jack asked.

"There." Knowles pointed ahead. A house sat at the edge of a crossroads, big, old and looking like its best days were several decades ago. Ivy clung to the front, and the roof held a mixture of different shades of grey tiles. The window frames needed paint, but the front door looked heavy and secure. The building was at the south side of the crossroads, opposite the road which led to Jack's old house.

The sun was sinking behind them, bathing everything in golden hour light. The streets were quiet. Not even a car moved. Somehow the neighbours hadn't come to see what the fuss was about with the helicopter. *Probably assumed it was the air ambulance.*

Knowles held up a hand, and they all stopped. He pointed at Miller and Penfold and then at the south of the house. Both nodded and ran into position. They were covering the only other way out of the house, just in case.

"Stay here," Knowles said to Jack and Bailey. "Wait until its clear. Towner, with me."

"Sir."

"What are you going to do?" Bailey said.

"I'm going to knock."

2

Knowles rapped hard on the door. *Rat tat. Rat tat tat. Rat tat tat tat.* He drew his Glock and held it behind his back. Towner braced against the wall besides the door, out of view of anyone who opened it.

No-one did.

He tried again. *Rat tat. Rat tat tat. Rat tat tat tat.*

Knowles pushed at the door, tried the handle. Nothing. No response. The house loomed in front of him, oppressive in its desire to keep its secrets. "Break it down" he said. Towner nodded and fired once at the lock. Kicking solid wood doors down was one for fantasists. The bang shattered the silence, sending birds scattering from the roof, squawking warnings as they flew away. The door swung open as the lock shattered. Towner led the way, weapon braced against his shoulder, barrel aimed into the hallway.

The stillness of the house hit him as wrong as soon as Knowles crossed the threshold. He swung the Glock into a ready position in front of him.

Towner slid into the living room, sweeping it quickly and moving through to the kitchen. "Sir!" he yelled.

Knowles had been about to go upstairs when he heard Towner's shout and he sprinted to his side. Four corpses lay in a neat line on the floor. Three had gaping cavities in their midriffs, and the last had a neat bullet hole in the middle of her forehead.

Kenny. Sandeman. Wijnberg. Howells.

"Shit." Knowles said, kneeling next to Kenny's body first and touching her cold skin. "Check upstairs, then get the others in here."

"Sir." Towner was considerably paler and less cocky than he had been on the flight over. He left the room, no doubt grateful for the fresher air out of the kitchen-come-crypt.

"I'm sorry," Knowles said to the four corpses. More people he'd sent to their deaths. More blood on his hands.

"Sir!"

He made his way upstirs, following Towner's shout. Towner was outside a room full of monitoring equipment. Inside, blood spattered the walls and computer screens. On the floor, surrounded by yet more blood lay a young man, his throat ripped out and the lower half of his face missing. Wide eyes stared at the ceiling, full of shock. Alex Thorne.

"Fuck."

"What now, sir?" Panic was clear in Towner's voice. The tremble in his hands, the break on the word 'now'.

"We stay calm is what now." Knowles ran a hand through his hair. "Somebody is missing. Potter. There's only five corpses, so our priority just became finding Potter."

"Sir, what about Stadler's kid?"

Knowles nodded. "Yeah, him too. If he's here."

Towner didn't move, kept his gaze on Thorne's corpse.

"You okay?"

Towner nodded, a slow deliberate action. "I don't want to get eaten, sir."

"Me neither, Towner, me neither."

"You've faced these things before sir. What do we do?"

"Shoot first," Knowles said. "Fuck the questions, fuck the doubt. Shoot and put them down. All of them."

3

They were in the garden, sat on the grass making plans. Penfold stood at the gate to the garden, watching the street and road in case anyone approached. No-one did. Miller was inside, trying to see what records the computers had.

"They could be long gone by now," Bailey said.

"Yeah, maybe." Knowles didn't sound convinced.

"Why take out your team?" Jack said. "What would that gain them? They'd know you'd come and get revenge. Maybe Bailey is right, and they've gone. Maybe they know of more wolves nearby and have gone for sanctuary."

"Not all wolves are bad." Knowles drummed his fingers on his knee. *Do you believe that? Really believe it?* "This doesn't look good, but what is the aim? Why do this, knowing what we'd do?"

"What if they wanted us here? What if *this* is what it gains them?" Bailey pointed at Knowles. "They get to take out the great wolf hunter, way to make themselves heroes in the wolf world."

"There aren't many wolves left in the UK," Knowles said.

"Because of you, sir." Towner saluted, somehow managing to make it look sarcastic, despite appearing genuine in his words.

Jack watched the exchange, lips terse. He kept his own counsel though: he was not here to question Knowles' actions. *That* reckoning would have to wait. Jack had never wanted this life, had only ever wanted a quiet easy existence with Katie and Josh. All of that had been wrenched from him ten years ago, but they'd managed to endure and keep together as a family.

And now, all had gone to shit again.

Depression opened its tremendous maw under him once more, and he felt himself falling, falling into its terrible blackness. *Katie. Katie.*

Katie. He just wanted to hold her; tell her how much he loved her; how lucky he was they'd ever met; how she made him a better person just by *being*.

Josh.

The thought of his son arrested the tumble into darkness. Josh needed help. Needed to be returned to his family, or what was left of it. Jack forced himself to think about Josh, to focus on his face. He didn't want him in danger for a second longer. The people who took him would suffer.

He stood up, making the others jump.

"What are you doing?" Knowles said.

"Stretching my legs." Jack walked to the gate and pushed past Penfold.

"Jack, wait," Knowles called, running after him. "We need to stick together."

Jack stopped in the street, gazing down at his old house. What was it like now? Who lived there? What had they changed? Did they know people had died there?

"No, Knowles. You lot need to stick together. I'll be fine."

"You're my responsibility." Knowles put a hand on his shoulder.

Jack laughed. "No, Knowles. Not even close. Stay out of my way."

"Jack," Bailey called. He held something in his hand, a look of surprise on his face.

"I mean it." Jack kept walking, crossing the road before he started to jog. He had no clue where he was headed as he ran past his old house and down the hill. As the old, familiar, pavements passed under the slap of his feet, he realised he was heading for the woods. His old running route, which had started this in the first place.

Somehow, that felt right, and he upped his pace, running down the hill.

4

"Where's he going?" Penfold said.

"I don't think even he knows," Knowles said. "He's hurting."

"Isn't everybody?"

Knowles didn't answer. "Take Miller and Towner. Follow him. Keep in touch though, okay? We don't know the others have actually left. They could be lurking somewhere."

"Yes sir." Penfold jogged away, going to get the others. Knowles beckoned Bailey over and headed back to the field.

Bailey caught him up. "What's going on?"

"Your friend has gone rogue."

"He's not—" Bailey began, but then changed his mind. "You asked me to watch him, to get close. Of course he's my friend."

"This has hit him hard."

Bailey grunted in response. "For fuck's sake, Knowles, he's just lost his wife. His son could go the same way. Were you expecting rainbow shitting unicorns?"

They were in the field with the helicopter, and the pilot waved at them. Knowles acknowledged him rather than answer Bailey. Truth was he was embarrassed at his failures so far this week. Failure to keep the entire team alive in London and Devon. Failure to keep Katie alive. Failure to keep Josh safe.

Katie was not his responsibility, but still, he felt her death as keenly as those of his own friends. He clicked the radio and put the call in. Two teams, ready to scramble at a moment's notice. High priority. Bailey listened in to the conversation, surprise on his face.

"You think they're still here? Surely they bugged out after doing this?"

Knowles nodded. "Maybe. I don't know. The bones are here, buried over there." He waved at the forest stretching over the nearest hill.

"The bones?"

"This all started when Jack fell on a bone. Remember Bryant? That arsehole deliberately spiked himself with one so he would also turn into an Original."

"I thought he was trying to cure his cancer?"

"The cancer he kept a secret from everyone? Yeah, okay. Turns out if you're a dick, then becoming an Original makes you more of a dick. Jack always used to talk about there being an almost constant argument inside him, with the Wolf wanting out." He ran a hand through his hair. "Jack could keep him under check most of the time."

"Him?" Bailey chuckled at Knowles choice of pronoun for the Wolf. "Okay, then. I'd go for it, but whatever man."

Knowles conceded the point. "I haven't seen the guy in ten years. Last time, he could control the Wolf. I'm not sure his anger and grief are helping."

"When we were in the pub, when those guys approached him. That's the only time I've seen him even come close to losing his shit. Until then, I—" He paused, not making eye contact with Knowles.

"Until then you thought it was bullshit?"

A reluctant nod.

"I get that a lot." Knowles gave him a grim smile. "I've seen a lot of strange things in the last ten years, Bailey." He didn't expand but sat in one of the rear seats of the helicopter. The pilot was reading a book, *A Quiet Apocalypse* by someone called Dave Jeffery. *Jesus, as if there's not enough horror in the world.*

"This is fucking great," the pilot said, as if sensing Knowles' distaste.

Knowles eventually looked at Bailey, hoping his face didn't betray the way he was feeling. "I need a win, Bailey. I need to find Josh and get him back to his dad. I can't lose anyone else to these things. To *any* things. You understand?"

Bailey did. He fiddled with something, turning it over and over in his hands.

"What is that?"

"Jack's phone. To be honest, with all this going on, I forgot I had it. He dropped it on the train, when he –" Bailey paused, colour fading from his cheeks. "When he changed."

Knowles took it from him and looked at it. The lock screen pinged into view with the usual app notifications present.

Step counted.

Weather.

Something called *Parent Tracker*.

"Can you unlock this?"

"Sure," Bailey said and typed Jack's code in. "Looks like all that spying did pay off."

Knowles clicked on the app and a map appeared, with a circle bouncing on a location. The circle had the picture of a smiling boy in it, and Knowles could immediately see the resemblance to Jack.

Josh.

The map showed Huntleigh.

5

Jack was halfway down the hill when he realised the soldiers were following him. He looked over his shoulder at them, scowling, but didn't stop or even slow down. He knew they'd be able to keep pace with him, knew they had stamina in their legs from years of training – even the one who looked about twelve.

He could let the Wolf out—

Please oh yes please please plea—

—but that was a non-starter. He was not ready to relinquish control to that just yet.

You're no fun anymore, Jack. Haven't been for a long time.

Maybe it was because the Wolf was closer to the surface than it had been in years and maybe it was just his mind playing tricks on him, but he caught a trace of a very familiar scent. He skidded to a halt, next to a driveway he must have passed hundreds of times and not noticed. A small sign had been screwed into a gate. *Plough Mill.*

Yes Jack. You're not imagining it.

He went to the gate and touched the sign. Just wood, letters painted on. Maybe this gate hadn't been there when he lived in Huntleigh. It was ten years ago after all. The gate was far taller than him, heavy solid wood painted a very dark brown. It blocked all view of anything behind it. Whoever had built it clearly wanted to preserve their privacy.

"Jack."

He turned to the voice. It was the twelve-year-old: Miller.

"We should get back to Captain Knowles," he said. The other two nodded, imploring him with their eyes. Jack understood then: the soldiers were scared. Not just of the situation, and the wolves, but more specifically, they were scared of *him*.

He didn't like that, but the Wolf did. The Wolf liked it very much.

"My son," Jack said, not making any move towards them. "He's here."

CHAPTER 14

1

Miller took his radio out and called Knowles. "Stadler says he's found his boy."

"We know!" Knowles sounded like he was running.

"House, bottom of the hill, near a big ass gate," Miller paused. "Wait, you know?"

"Don't go any further, Miller! Don't let Jack go."

"Yes sir." *How the hell am I supposed to stop him?* He didn't voice his thought, just stowed the radio instead. "Knowles said to wait here."

Jack touched the gate, giving no indication he'd heard Miller. He couldn't see a latch, or padlock, or in fact anyway to open the gate. Turning, he looked at the short driveway again, and saw a keypad on a metal pole near Towner.

"Tight security for Devon," he said.

"Mr Stadler, uh, Jack," Miller said, "Knowles wants us to wait."

"Yeah, I'm sure he does." Jack inspected the keypad, seeing it had a tiny camera built into the top of it. "But it's not his son in there."

He ran and jumped at the gate, fingers gripping the top and he pulled himself up and over in one smooth movement.

"Well, shit," Miller said.

2

Jack landed, rolled straight into a crouch. He could see a large tree, so he ran to it, hiding until he got his bearings. To his left, a large barn dominated the land, and beyond that he could see a track leading to the woods. The driveway continued round to his right, with another, smaller barn set back from the drive. Opposite that, three cars sat in an open area surrounded by a rickety looking fence.

Two of the cars looked beat up, but the last was a top of the range Range Rover with this year's plates. A sure sign, if the size of the grounds and barns weren't, that the owners were very, very wealthy. Jack crouched again and ran to the nearest of the older cars – a Clio – then elongated a finger, the nail turning into a claw. He jabbed it into the tyre and ripped the rubber open before repeating the action with every other tyre. The three cars sank lower as the air rushed out of the ruined rubber.

"You're not getting away," he whispered to himself.

He could see the house at the very end of the driveway, surrounded by trees. It was much larger than he'd expected, but long and narrow. A proper old Devon longhouse. Bits had clearly been added over time, giving the house an unusual footprint. A conservatory pulled the house into a L-shape, with another extension at the tip of the L. Glass doors sat in the middle of the house, not far from the side of the conservatory.

Jack couldn't see any movement inside. *Doesn't mean a thing.*

There was little cover between where he was and the house. He had no choice but to run straight across. Jack took and deep breath and sprinted across the garden.

3

Knowles and Bailey ran down the hill, stopping when they saw the others. "Where's Jack?"

"He jumped the fence, sir." Miller didn't look happy, but whether that was at *telling* Knowles Jack had not listened, or Jack's actual actions, was unclear.

"What is this place?"

"Plough Mill," Towner said and held his phone up. "Sold about three years ago. Plans are still online – look."

They could see the floor plan of the long house.

"Christ, that's a lot of bottle necks and choke points," Knowles said.

"We have superior fire power, sir." Penfold held her rifle up as if Knowles didn't know what she was talking about.

"They have at least one hostage. They are also wolves." A knot was developing in Knowles' stomach again. The one full of worry, full of fear. "Do not under-estimate them. Remember Rawson."

Penfold looked at her feet. "Sir," she muttered.

"Ok, Miller, Towner, I need you two to circle in from the North of the house. Head for this door," he pointed at a doorway on the floorplan, around the other side of the house near the imposing fence circling the property. "Be quiet though. We sneak, no weapons unless we have to. As soon as you have eyes on the door, hunker down and watch. Anything that comes out that isn't Jack or his boy is put down. Understand?" He waited long enough for the other two to confirm.

"Bailey, Penfold, head for the conservatory. You're looking to block the exits. The longer they don't know we're here, the more chance we all get to walk out of here."

"What about you?" Bailey said.

"I'm going to find Jack and try and keep him calm and safe until the back-up arrives."

"Back-up?" Miller looked confused.

"We don't need no back-up." Towner, overconfident, as usual.

"For fuck's sake," Penfold rolled her eyes.

Knowles gave him a hard stare. "Stop being a dick, Towner. You know these *things* have killed people. You saw what they did to Kenny and the others. We need to be at our best." He looked at his watch. "We have two teams on their way from Chivenor. ETA is not for another thirty minutes minimum, more likely forty-five. Let's hope they're not needed."

"Can we wait for them to arrive?" Miller was very pale.

"That was the plan," Knowles admitted, "but Jack has kind of screwed that. We get in there, try and contain this. Hold the exit points of the house. No-one leaves. Got it?"

They all nodded.

"Okay, stay safe, watch each other's backs, and we'll get through this."

4

Potter and Josh crept along the tunnel. Burnt husks of spider crunched underfoot and the air held the acrid stench of burnt flesh. Meagre torchlight struggled to illuminate the gloom ahead whilst Potter tried, and failed, to focus on the journey. Every step was torture, expecting spiders to drop from the ceiling, scuttle out of the cracks in the walls, cover them both in seconds, their questing legs probing every orifice, finding entry points in nose and mouth and –

He shuddered. The kid just walked along with a blank expression on his face. He didn't seem at all bothered by the thought of the spiders returning. Truth told, he didn't seem bothered by anything. Did he even know he wasn't going to be alive for much longer? Potter swallowed the thought. Killing the team had been easy – they were such annoying righteous bastards. Murdering a kid? A whole new ball game.

Potter's father had always used that phrase, for anything. Going to college? Whole new ball game. Getting a girlfriend for more than a month? Joining the military? Whole new ball game. First posting abroad? First time in conflict? Whole new ball game. Aggressive, inoperable stomach cancer that ate his father away in a matter of months? Whole new ball game.

Despite facing death more times than he could remember, cancer was the thing that terrified Potter the most. Whenever he pictured his father, emaciated, pale and unable to stand alone, his own legs went weak. *I'm not going out like that.* Soon after his father's funeral, he'd been on base in the UK, hearing crazy stories about wolves and how one of their own had flipped to become one in order to cure his cancer.

Potter dug deeper, finding the truth in the stories. From there, it had been easy to arrange a transfer to Knowles' team and then to the Huntleigh crew. Becoming a wolf would prevent an illness like his father's. The doctors had advised him to get checked every year as the cancer was hereditary. Small risk, they said, statistically unlikely. But that was the thing about statistics, wasn't it? It happened to someone. He was in the clear at the moment, but it was only a matter of time. Potter was literally his own ticking time bomb. Of course he'd read Bryant's file and he understood the risks.

Not me. Not like that.

The tunnel opened into a cavern slightly larger than the one they'd left. No other tunnels left this one, boulders blocking any exits that might once have existed. A large skull lay on the floor near the centre, empty eye sockets regarding them without emotion.

"Pick it up," Potter said. Something about it screamed *Go. Don't touch. Leave this place.*

Josh went to it without a word and lifted it up. It was an off white, almost yellow, but was that due to the torch light? The snout had a full set of long teeth set along the jaw. The front canines were a few inches long, clearly designed for ripping and shredding food.

"Wow," Potter said, swallowing revulsion and fear. The kid didn't look bothered, and no way was Potter letting some snotty little shit get the upper hand. "That's amazing."

Josh remained impassive. "Can we go now? I don't like it down here."

Almost on cue, they heard a soft rustle behind them. A scratch of leg on rock. A chittering scrape of carapace on carapace. Potter looked to where the other tunnels had collapsed. Thick black legs poked through miniscule gaps in the rockfall. A spider emerged, then another and another until there were too many to count. It was like a spider dam had burst and they swarmed over the wall, turning it black despite the torchlight.

Potter had no idea if there were more bones down here than the skull, but he didn't care either. The sight and sound of the spiders made his skin crawl.

"Run!"

5

Jordan sat in the kitchen, with her mother. They both had untouched glasses of wine in front of them, neither really feeling the need to drink but pouring them out of habit. For her part, Jordan was a little sad that Alex was dead – he'd been a great shag, after all. Nothing more than a means to an end. She had thought maybe he would join them once he discovered everything they were planning, but her mum put paid to that. *Probably just as well.*

Everything was for the good of the pack.

Five words drummed into her since she'd been a little girl: *the good of the pack*. Nothing else mattered. Still, at night, just as she closed her eyes, she did wonder when she'd be allowed to start her own pack. Her mother wouldn't have been much older than Jordan was now when she'd started. Back in those days, when Emilia and Rich had joint control, joint leadership. Then, a decade or so ago, it all came crashing down when the public found out about the wolves.

Her mum discovered where the Original had come from – Jordan wasn't sure how. She and Uncle Rich argued about the legitimacy of the stories, but Emilia won and so here they were, stuck in the middle of nowhere.

And now they were all to be Originals. Maybe. Possibly. Her mother was adamant the bones were there, close to the house. Jordan had been pushed into Engineering, *for the good of the pack*. She had a natural aptitude for the subject, however, so it hadn't been a hard push. The tunnel had used every bit of her expertise, and it was exciting to see her theory in practice. Perhaps she should write a thesis on the tunnel, show her studies in a practical and real-life situation. Would that be enough for a Masters? Would she want to return to Academia once she was an Original?

Jordan stretched and stood. She hated waiting for anything, but this seemed especially annoying. Movement to her side caught her attention. The security screen for the gate – installed during one of Emilia's more paranoid moments – showed something moving. Something that shouldn't be there.

"What's that?" She pointed at the screen.

Emilia came over, leaning in to get a closer look. On the screen, several figures were gathered in front of the gate. Four men. One woman. Three of the men and the woman in army fatigues. Another man looking like he'd just got up from a night out. The figures moved out of sight of the camera. Emilia leaned in and pressed some buttons.

The view changed. Now they were looking down at the gate, from their side of it. There were the figures, dropping onto the driveway. Two ran to one side, keeping low and heading around to the front of the house. The rest ran to where the cars were parked.

"Trouble," Emilia said, as she started to undress. "Go get your uncles. Quickly."

6

Knowles crept around the Clio, keeping low. The tyres were all slashed, but that was the only evidence of Jack he'd found so far. Bailey came with him, Penfold on the opposite side of the driveway. Bailey was sweating, face pale.

"You don't have to do this," Knowles said.

"Bit late, mate." Bailey flashed an unconvincing smile. "It seems I'm invested."

"Don't hesitate with your weapon."

"Not my first time, Knowles. You know me better than that."

No. I knew you were better than that years ago. Teaching PE doesn't exactly prepare you for a life and death fight.

"Where the fuck is he?"

Bailey didn't reply. There was no need. Jack was nowhere to be seen.

"Ready?"

Penfold leant on the side of the barn, aiming down the sights of her SA80. She held a hand up, then dropped it. Knowles and Bailey ran towards the house. The conservatory was below them, where the house sat in a dip. Knowles glanced at the length of the house, but he couldn't see any movement. Still, running across the garden like that would have them in full view of the inhabitants for far too long.

Being quick was a shit plan, but it was the only one they had.

He and Bailey sprinted into the garden.

7

Jordan swept her phone off the counter and speed-dialled Rich's latest number on his burner. He answered after the first ring.

"We've got company," she said and hung up. Turning back to the kitchen, she could see two men running across the garden. "Shit!"

She started to take her clothes off, and then her mother, her glorious, beautiful mother sprinted out of the house as a wolf, heading straight for the two men.

8

"Holy fuck!" Bailey roared as a large brown wolf burst out of the conservatory. He skidded to a halt, turning away as the wolf crossed the gap between them in a few steps.

"Move!" Knowles said, trying to bring the Glock to bear, but he didn't have a shot. Bailey was in the way.

Bailey heard the fear in Knowles' voice and raised his SA80. It felt like moving through treacle compared to the speed of the wolf. He heard the roar of bullets screaming from Penfold's weapon behind him, but the wolf zig-zagged, sidestepping with a grace that belied its size.

Less than five metres away.

It pounced.

Something hit it in mid-air. A bigger wolf.

A much bigger Wolf.

The collision sent them sprawling in mass of fur and snapping teeth. The Wolf found its footing first and it opened its enormous mouth, closing it around the other creature's neck. It shook the wolf like a dog with a squeaky toy, and blood spurted out of the wound.

The wolf emitted a high pitch howl, which soon changed to a whine and a whimper. It thrashed for a moment even as the Wolf bit down hard. Harder.

Harder still.

Bailey heard bones snap and then the wolf stopped moving.

9

Jordan saw her mother die. Her throat ripped to shreds in seconds by
that monstrosity.

"NO!"

10

Chris heard the scream before he left the tunnel. It sounded like
Jordan, and panic gripped him. Despite the cold feeling spreading
through his gut and legs, he accelerated, feet pounding on rock and
then tiles. Up the stairs and out into the house, Rich close behind.

Jordan, half undressed, lay on the floor, screaming and bawling her
eyes out. She saw him and raised a feeble hand to point. He followed
and felt his own cry rising.

"Emilia!" Rich roared.

Chris grabbed his arm and held fast. "You go out there, you'll get
killed too."

Rich pulled and thrashed, but his brother held firm.

"We take them out, one at a time."

"Emilia!" Rich's voice cracked, then shattered as he dissolved into
cries. Chris held him fast, not letting him attack the soldiers approaching the house.

"Easy, fella," Chris said. He looked at Jordan, who was still hysterical on the floor. Normally her state of undress would cause him
problems, but not today. He slapped her.

Her look of shock was comical as she held a hand against her cheek.

"Get Rich to the tunnel. Get him out of here. He's no use to
anyone in this state." She didn't move, just sat there, glass eyed and red

cheeked. "Fuck's sake, girl, now, move your arse!" His words got her moving and she helped Rich to his feet. Chris watched as they headed back to the pantry and down into the tunnels.

He could see the soldiers in the garden, with a naked man who he recognised at once. "Holy shit, it's Jack fucking Stadler," Chris whispered.

Something shifted behind him, and Chris spun, keeping low. He was looking at the front door, that led out directly to the road, or it would, were it not behind another huge wooden fence. Emilia really liked her privacy. Chris waited, knowing his wolf senses hadn't deceived him: there were more people that way.

A soldier edged into view, walking slowly in a crouch. If it weren't for the stench coming from him, Chris wouldn't have known he was there. He scrambled across the hallway, ending underneath the window so he was out of sight.

He waited.

11

Penfold aimed the weapon at Jack. He knew she didn't mean to, that it was only natural, but it still pissed him off. The Wolf chuckled, even as he banished it back down. Deep down, wherever it went.

"Relax," he said. Penfold's eyes widened, and Jack winced. "Not my best choice of words, sorry."

"Holy shit, Jack." Bailey couldn't take his eyes off the corpse at Jack's feet. He didn't think he'd ever seen such a short, one-sided fight.

"Recognise it?" Knowles was, of course, all business.

Jack shook his head. "I don't know many wolves, Knowles, you know that."

"Where are the others?" Penfold had, at last, stopped aiming the weapon at Jack. Instead, she was aiming at the conservatory.

"We're sitting ducks out here," Knowles said. "Get cover, then let's approach the house."

They spread out, though there was very little in the garden to hide their approach. Only Jack stood tall, his lips twisted in a sneer.

They heard a distant scream and then gunfire.

Jack was off and running before anyone else could react.

12

The front door swung open with a force that caught Miller by surprise. Then a wolf leapt out of the shadows, hitting him square in the chest. Miller fell backwards under the force of the blow, hitting the deck as the wolf snapped down with its teeth. Somehow it missed his arm, and then all the pressure was off his chest as the wolf ran at Towner.

Too slow.

Towner was too slow.

He didn't even get a round off as the wolf leapt at him. Towner was stronger than Miller, so he only staggered under the assault. He didn't fall, which was what killed him. The wolf bit Towner's arm, dragging its teeth the length of his forearm, opening a dozen wounds. Towner screamed and screamed until the wolf released his arm and tore his throat out instead.

Miller knelt up, staring down his sights, just as the wolf spun Towner, blocking Miller's shot. Towner's screams had stopped, but he was still clinging to life even if it wasn't going to be for much longer.

Shoot them both.

Blood splashed out of Towner's mouth, covering the wolf.

He's dead he's dead he's dead—

The Wolf tossed Towner's corpse to the side, as casually as throwing a jacket on a sofa after a hard day at work.

Shoot the fucking wolf.

But no wolf stood in front of Miller anymore. Just a man. A large naked man. Miller paused, even though he knew. Despite everything, despite all the training, despite all the shit he'd seen, he paused when he saw a human.

A human holding Towner's weapon.

13

The Wolf leapt at the conservatory, shattering glass, and taking the window frame with him. It landed, paws struggling to gain purchase for a moment, but then it was running through the house, following the other wolf's scent.

He found it stood over a dead man, holding a weapon. It was in its inferior human state and the Wolf laughed to itself as it charged into the stupid human. Bullets tore into the Wolf, but it didn't care as it opened its enormous jaws around the man's head.

Pain roared up its side as more bullets poured into its flesh, but it didn't relinquish its hold. It pulled and bit with one action, and the man's head popped off the body with a wet squelch. Bullets continued to scream out of the weapon as the body's arms and legs shook and quivered, not seeming to realise their host was already dead.

The Wolf twisted to look at its side, seeing the damage there and it sank to its haunches, then to the ground. Fire raced up its side, and it whimpered.

We've been shot.

No shit Jackie boy.

We'll be okay, right? Not the first time we've been shot.

Hurts Jack. Everything hurts.

The Wolf lay its enormous head on the naked corpse and closed its eyes.

14

Rich and Jordan headed into the tunnels, leaning on each other, more for emotional support than any physical need. Both still had tears streaming down their face, but at least they were moving.

"Emilia," Rich said, his voice a notch above a whisper. He felt empty, numb, cold and yet hot. His legs felt as though they belonged to someone else as he made his way along the corridor, Jordan helping hold him up. Or maybe he was holding her up? He wasn't sure of anything now.

"Rich?" Harry stood in the cavern waiting for Josh and Potter's return. Somewhere behind them, they heard gunfire. Screams. More gunfire. Harry's face was creased into a frown.

"Emilia." Rich couldn't manage anything more.

"Where's Chris?"

"He stayed to fight the soldiers," Jordan said.

There was no emotion in her voice. She sounded like a bad actor reciting lines.

"Soldiers?" Harry said. He was about to say more when they heard the rush of footsteps down the tunnel.

Potter and Josh both ran into the cavern, panting hard. Potter paused, one hand on his thighs, sweat pouring down his forehead, doubled over with the effort of breathing. Josh was also out of breath, but still eyed Rich with a combination of fear and disgust.

"Did you get it?" Rich said, his voice thick with anger and grief.

Potter heaved to get air into his lungs. "Spiders, man. The spiders are back."

Rich pushed him against the wall, holding him there as easily as if he were a child. His fingers elongated into claws, their tips pressing against Potter's neck.

Harry peered into the tunnel and there, sure enough, were the skittering forms of the hideous spiders. He stepped back and hit something with his foot. A clink of glass on rock as the bottle rolled away told him what it was. He scooped up the last remaining bottle of whiskey, then pulled a lighter from his pocket.

"Fire in the hole!"

He lit the rag and hurled the bottle into the tunnel. Flames raced up the tunnel walls, igniting the chasing spiders in a blazing inferno.

"Did you get it?" Rich said, voice rising with each word and dragging Harry's attention back to the room.

Potter had his breathing back under control, but was pale and sweating, trying to pull away from Rich's claws "The kid has it."

Rich let him go, turning to Josh as if seeing him for the first time. At his feet sat a large skull and the boy took a step back from it. The skull was easily bigger than his own head, with a long snout and huge teeth embedded in its jaws. It was smooth – no cracks on it at all – which struck him as odd. Maybe there was something to the stories after all.

He hunkered down next to it.

"Soldiers are coming," Rich said. "They killed Emilia."

"It wasn't the soldiers. It was one of us." Jordan's eyes welled up again, and she sobbed. She buried her face in her hands and wept, anguished cries too loud and harsh for the confined space.

"That wasn't one of *us*. The wolf was enormous. Biggest I've ever seen. It was *him*."

Harry didn't need to know who Rich meant. He bit but the urge to say, "I told you."

Without another word, Rich slapped his hand down onto one of the big teeth. He winced as the tooth slid into his hand. Blood ran down the tooth, along the line of bone and pooling on the floor underneath the skull. Rich refused to show anyone how much it hurt, instead pulling his hand back up, removing his hand from the tooth with a wet pop. He examined the wound, tracing it with a finger.

"Well?" Potter's eyes gleamed in the glow of burning spiders.

Rich slammed his hand down again, making the hole in his hand bigger. He hit again, and again. Each strike made fresh blood splash out, but still Rich didn't cry out. Eventually, he stopped, and stared at his ruined hand. He tried to make a fist, but his hand wouldn't obey, but trembled as blood continued to pour out.

"Nothing," he said. "Fucking nothing." He snapped the tooth out, holding it to the light. Thick red blood coated it.

"Maybe it takes time," Harry said, and Rich leapt to his feet, fist moving at the same time. Harry pushed his damaged hand away easily, his own arm becoming coated with Rich's blood in the process. "Don't," he said.

"These bones made two Originals," Potter said. "Stadler and Bryant. Bryant hit his hand on the bones, and it took several hours to work. He drove all the way from here back to Kent and no-one he travelled with knew anything. Jack was impaled though. He should've died instantly, but he didn't."

"Are you saying we need to kill ourselves for this to work?" Even in his state, Rich still managed to exude menace from every pore.

Potter shook his head. "No, I'm agreeing with Harry. I think it takes time, but we can maybe speed it up by doing more damage."

Rich sank back to the ground, curling up and hugging himself. "Hurts." It was probably the first time in his life he'd ever admitted to being in pain. He rocked on the floor, moaning to himself.

"We don't have time," Harry said, eyes wide. "Those soldiers will kill us all before we get a chance for this to work. We have minutes, not hours."

"Yeah," Rich said, and he unfurled himself, lunging forward and swiping at Potter. He imbedded the tooth in Potter's neck, slamming it through flesh and muscle. Blood spurted out of the hole, spraying the wall next to Potter.

Potter screamed and put his hands to his neck, but it was too late. The damage was done. He collapsed, still holding his neck as more and more blood spurted out. Rich leant over him and pulled the tooth out of the wound with a wet sucking sound.

"Jesus, Rich," Harry said.

"Your turn," Rich said, gasping whilst he clenched and unclenched his hand. He handed the tooth to Harry. "Die by bullet when those soldiers get here, or maybe become a god. Your choice."

Harry swallowed; his mouth dry. Potter lay still on the floor, not moving, but not losing any more blood either. He couldn't have bled out already, could he? Harry looked at Potter's chest but couldn't see any movement. Then, a slight upward movement. Tiny, almost imperceptible, but Potter was definitely breathing. Did that mean it had worked?

He heard the skittering, scraping noise signifying the approach of the spiders. He didn't want to look at the tunnel to confirm it. The sound was awful enough, without seeing the hateful things. Spiders behind him, soldiers in front, and somewhere in the middle of all this a really, really pissed off Original.

He had no choice.

Harry slammed the tooth into his neck and then dropped it as soon as blood erupted from the wound. He grunted and collapsed, lying next to Potter. His blood spread on the ground, mingling with Potter's.

Rich retrieved the tooth with his good hand. He glanced at Jordan, standing as far away from the spiders' tunnel as she could. "Join us," he said. "Join us."

He cut his own neck open.

15

Josh was the only person in the cavern who made no move to the skull. He edged away from the tunnel opening, keeping quiet whilst they were all pre-occupied. He slipped behind Rich, waiting for a hand on his shoulder, a cry, a warning. None came. The other tunnel led back to the house, and he could see the length of it. Not far to the house. Not far to sanctuary, away from these mad people. Still expecting pain to hit him as he was struck from behind, Josh took off, sprinting down the tunnel as fast as his legs could carry him.

16

"He'll be fine," Knowles said.

Penfold had her SA80 aimed at the row of corpses. Miller. Towner. *Jesus.* A third body lacked a head and was entirely naked. Next to that one lay a huge Wolf. She knew it was Jack Stadler; knew what they were dealing with, but it still shocked her to see it.

Jack wasn't moving, and his fur was soaked with blood, making his grey/brown fur almost black.

"Who's that?" Bailey brought up the rear, aiming his weapon into the depths of the house.

"At a guess, it's one of the brothers." Knowles pointed at the big corpse. "Which one is kind of hard to say until we find his head."

"Do you think Jack, uh, ate—"

"Probably best not to continue that line of thought, Bailey," Knowles said.

Penfold turned and threw up, splashing vomit over Towner and her own shoes. She stopped long enough to look horrified, then threw up some more. After a few empty gags and retches, she stood, wiping her mouth with the back of her hand.

"Sorry," she said.

"We've all been there." Knowles gave her a kind and sympathetic smile. "You okay?"

She nodded and hoisted her weapon into a 'ready' position.

"We've seen the plans of this place," Knowles said. "Check down here first, then clear upstairs. No heroics. Check your sixes. Everyone stays in sight, clear?"

"What about him?" Bailey pointed at the Wolf.

"We don't have time to wait. Let's get his boy."

17

Jordan's eyes flicked from the skull to the tunnel to the three prone men. Something moved behind her, but she couldn't take her eyes from the scene in front of her. There was a lot of blood in the cavern, but even Rich had stopped bleeding. How long does it take to bleed out from a neck wound? She had no idea, but guessed it was seconds rather than minutes. All three were still breathing – barely, but still alive.

"Fuck," she said.

Wait. Where's the kid?

She realised what the other movement she'd seen was. The fucking kid was escaping and with him, their insurance against the soldiers. With a roar, she set off after him.

18

Knowles took point, Bailey in the middle, Penfold at the rear. They made their way down a short corridor that led to an office on the left, with steps down to a pantry on the right. *A pantry? Who the fuck has a pantry these days?* Ahead, the corridor continued for a few more metres until it opened into a large living room.

Knowles slid into the room, sweeping the area with his weapon and confirming it was empty. He made a twirling gesture with his hand, indicating to turn around. Bailey nodded and did the same to Penfold.

As they turned, they all heard the *pat pat pat* of approaching footsteps. No words passed between them. Penfold knelt. Bailey braced against the left-hand wall. Knowles took the right.

Each aimed down their sights, fingers ready on triggers.

pat pat pat

The footsteps came closer and closer.

19

Josh was sure the tunnel hadn't been as long when they'd first come along it. Like most ten-year-olds, he could run and run, but today his legs felt wobbly and his chest hurt. Maybe the added pressure of running for your life drained your energy faster? Josh couldn't focus on anything, other than keeping his feet moving, one in front of the other.

Don't stop. Don't trip. Don't fall.

He wasn't an athletic boy at all, much preferring PlayStation and books to sports, but as a family they walked for miles each weekend. He was light, skinny and, as it turned out, fast.

Finally, *there*, at last, came the end of the tunnel. He burst into the pantry and hurtled up the stairs, nearly tripping in his eagerness to climb them. His feet clumped on the wooden steps, the noise thudding and loud in the confines of the small room.

At the top of the stairs, he yanked the door open and headed into the house. He lost his footing on the tiled floor, feet sliding from underneath him, pitching him forward, even as he heard more noise behind him.

Someone was coming after him.

And they were close.

20

Jordan could see the little shit in front of her, just as he disappeared up the stairs. He was their protection, their safety net, their insurance against the soldiers just killing them all. She had to get him back into the caves.

She heard him run up the stairs, his feet hitting the steps with the grace of a duckling. A misstep, a slip. Had he fallen? She entered the pantry in time to see him open the door and she leapt at him, wolf bursting out of her.

21

The shape in the doorway exploded into the corridor and all three opened fire. Bullets streamed into the corridor, with many smacking straight into the walls, tearing books apart on the bookshelf and ripping apart the open door.

A wolf stood in the corridor, snarling at something on the floor and the bullets tore into its flank. It howled and whimpered as the constant rain forced it back along the corridor.

"Cease fire!" Knowles roared. *Oh shit.* On the ground. In front of the wolf. A small boy in a t-shirt and jogging bottoms.

Josh.

Penfold and Bailey stopped shooting as Knowles pushed past them. "Secure this area," he roared, pointing at the ruined door. He knelt next to the boy, and checked him over. His heart thumped in his suddenly tight chest. Bullets had ruined the hallway, smashing apart all in their wake.

Josh rolled over and sat up, blinking at Knowles.

Christ.

"Josh?" Bailey said. He'd run to the door but stopped as soon as he saw the kid on the floor.

"Bailey!" Josh cried. "Is my dad with you?"

The wolf howled and thrashed on the floor, trying to get its back legs to work. Claws scrabbled on the wooden floor, gouging deep scratches out.

"No, you don't," Bailey said, aimed, and shot it in the head.

22

Every fibre of Rich's body felt like it was on fire. Had this happened to Stadler? Bryant? How long would this last. He managed to open his eyes to see Potter and Harry also on the floor, both curled into the foetal position.

In the distance, he heard gunshots and groaned.

The soldiers were coming.

23

Cordite hung heavy in the air, like smoke in a night club. Knowles toed the wolf corpse, but it didn't move. *Having your brains spread over a wall would do that.* "You okay, kid?"

Josh nodded. He was standing with Bailey, holding his hand. Bailey looked both happy and slightly awkward at that.

"Penfold, what can you see?"

When the shooting stopped, Penfold had moved to the ruined doorway, using the frame as cover.

"Nothing, sir. No movement here. Steps down to what looks like a tunnel."

"Where's my dad?"

Knowles ignored the boy. "Secure the tunnel, Penfold."

"Sir."

She disappeared, down the stairs, moving slowly so as not to give her position away.

"What's down there, Josh?"

"I want my mum."

Knowles' eye twitched. Did he know his mother was dead? Had he seen it? "Your dad is here, and Bailey will take you to him in a minute. Can you tell us what's down there first?"

Josh looked at Bailey, seeking some sort of affirmation that Knowles was actually okay. Bailey nodded and smiled. "This is Knowles, Squiggs. An old friend of your dad's. He's cool."

It was good enough for Josh. "It's a tunnel into a cave. We got chased by spiders."

Knowles shuddered. *Spiders.* A cold chill ran down his spine.

"How many people are down there? How many like that?" He pointed at the wolf.

"Four." Josh's face screwed up with concentration, then his eyes opened wider as he considered the wolf on the floor. "No, three."

"Thank you. Bailey will take you to your dad. We'll get you somewhere safe."

Bailey's face was full of questions, and he frowned. Knowles gave him a grim smile.

"Jack'll be fine," he said.

Bailey didn't look convinced, but he led Josh away anyway. Knowles took a deep breath, checked his rounds and followed Penfold.

24

He found Penfold at the mouth of a rough-hewn tunnel. Lights spaced evenly along the length illuminated the way, showing just how busy the wolves had been.

"Impressive," he whispered.

Penfold nodded. "Do you think they got the earth out like in the Great Escape?"

"*That's* what you're thinking of right now?"

She didn't reply, but walked carefully into the tunnel. It was too bright, when they were in the pools of illumination, and they both felt too exposed. Penfold kept her weapon aimed down the tunnel, scanning for targets, but nothing moved. They made slow, painful progress, creeping along and not trying to make any noise.

They'll know we're coming.

Knowles didn't want to say the wolves would smell them long before they saw them, but he couldn't see another solution here. They had to get the wolves and stop them getting through to the bones. He knew the spiders were drawn to Original bones – he had first-hand experience of that – so if they had found the spiders, then maybe the bones weren't too far behind.

Years before, they'd tried to destroy the bones, but nothing had worked, not even cremating them. Pulverising them with a hammer had worked the longest, but then they reformed anyway. Burying them in separate piles had been the only way.

And now that's about to bite them in the arse.

Penfold held her hand up. Something ahead. Knowles put a hand on her shoulder and pointed onwards. She nodded, lips a thin line, sweat beading on her forehead. Knowles could see why she'd paused. Three men lay on the ground ahead, surrounding something white which glinted in the torchlight.

What the hell?

They edged forward again, progress even slower than before. Closer now, Knowles could see the features of the men. One was Potter, and another was Rich Taylor, the original target back in London. A nasty, nasty man with a long trail of bodies behind him. He didn't know the third.

All three were coated in blood, but he couldn't see where the wounds were.

"Penfold," Knowles said. He was surprised at how calm he sounded.

"Sir?"

"Keep me covered."

25

"Daddy!"

Josh ran and jumped on Jack, holding him in a hug only a ten-year-old can give.

Jack looked groggy, but his face lit up when he saw his son, and he returned the hug as intensely as only a father can give.

"Where are your clothes daddy?"

"Not entirely sure, Squiggs," Jack said. He smiled at Bailey, his expression full of relief. "You okay?"

Bailey nodded. "Yeah. Weird day, huh?" Lots of coats hung from hooks by the front door, and Bailey threw a long duffel coat at Jack. "I've seen more of you than I want to, Jack."

Jack felt heat rush to his cheeks. "Sorry man."

"Where's mum?"

And like that, the relief and pleasure at seeing Josh evaporated. Jack's face fell, and tears welled in his eyes. Before he could say anything, stabbing pain roared through his gut, doubling him over. He gasped, clutching his stomach.

"Dad?"

"Jack?"

Jack moaned and groaned, holding his side where the bullets had hit. Shells littered the floor around him, pushed out as his body healed a few minutes before. He blinked, trying to bring the world into focus.

"You okay?" Bailey's face was full of concern.

Jack nodded. "I haven't been shot in a while, and that's the second time today." Just forgot how much it hurt, that's all. Is there anything to drink?"

26

I really am too old for this shit. Danny Glover's voice rang through Knowles' mind, even though he hadn't seen *Lethal Weapon* in over twenty years. His chest still felt tight, but he didn't want to think about that. *Just some anxiety. That's all.*

He edged closer to the three bodies, feeling no comfort at all knowing Penfold was watching his every move. None of them moved. Blood coated the ground around them, and their clothes, but he couldn't see any evidence of injury.

No wounds.

"Penfold," he said. "Get ready to run."

He knelt next to Potter, inspecting him more closely. No obvious wounds. Was he too late? Again?

"We need knives."

"Sir?"

He stood, edging away from the bodies on the ground. "We're going to have to cut their heads off."

"Sir?"

He didn't need to look at her: he heard the disgust in her voice.

"Have you got a knife?"

"Not one that'll do *that*."

"Okay. Run and get one. Bring Bailey back with you, and lots of explosives."

27

Jack was making him nervous. No two ways about it, nothing else to say, just his entire presence felt wrong. He sat in the kitchen, hugging his boy, and even that act of paternal love made Bailey itch.

Footsteps dragged his attention back to the pantry door – or at least, what remained of it. Penfold emerged from the wreckage, and ran past him, heading for the kitchen.

"Boss needs a knife," she yelled.

"What?"

"And explosives."

Bailey followed her, leaving Jack and Josh sitting in the large living room, talking quietly with each other. "What have you found?"

"Bodies. Three blokes. One of them is one of ours. Potter."

Bailey shrugged. "Never met the bloke. He dead?"

"Seems to be, but Knowles said get a knife so here I am. You going to help or what?"

"Help?"

"Get everyone's grenades."

Bailey looked at the line of corpses and his heart sank.

28

They still hadn't moved, which filled Knowles with relief. *They're not zombies, moron.* He was kneeling on the ground, watching them intently.

"Please stay dead," he whispered, but kept his weapon trained on the bodies nevertheless. "Please don't be what I think you are."

Muscles in his back and legs protested as he stood. Sweat dripped down his back, yet another sign he was, indeed, too old for this shit. He could put a bullet in each of their heads, but that might just draw the wolves out in defence. Better to wait for back up, and pray the fuckers didn't get up anyway.

29

Jack got as far as the kitchen door before he doubled over in pain. He clutched his stomach and fell to his knees with a shout.

"Dad!"

Bailey and Penfold ran into the room at the shout. Josh stood on a sofa, eyes wide at the sight of his father rolling on the floor clutching his stomach.

"Jack?" Bailey said. He moved towards Josh, giving Jack as wide a berth as was possible in the living room.

Sweat poured from Jack, soaking the coat he wore. It fell open, and they all saw his skin *moving*. Waves rippled across his stomach and down his legs, the flesh in constant motion. Black hairs burst from his flesh and Bailey recoiled.

"Get Josh out of here," Bailey screeched. Part of him felt a little ashamed at the high-pitched shout.

Jack threw back his head and howled.

30

Things moved in the distance, in the darkness further into the cave system. Knowles could hear them. A scrape of chitinous carcass on rock. A scuttle of limbs as spiders moved somewhere in the darkness beyond the cavern. He couldn't help picturing them crawling ever closer, coming towards him, coming to eat him—

Definitely time to put the papers in. Call it a day.

"Spiders," Knowles muttered. "Fucking spiders."

31

"Josh, here, now!" Bailey yelled holding his hand out and pulling the boy closer. His father was on all fours, back arched and still howling.

"Bailey, we need to go!" Penfold shouted. Panic coursed through her in ways it never had before – not even on mission. Stadler was changing, but not like before. Then, he'd seemed like he was in control. This was closer to pure, unadulterated rage.

We're in trouble here.

The ruined door to the pantry flapped in front of her but she pushed past it. Bailey and Josh were close behind, with Bailey holding tight as Josh tried to turn back to Jack. They were in the kitchen again.

"Let me go!" Josh cried, and then he screamed with anguish. "DAD!"

A flash of movement down the corridor made her gasp. An enormous wolf stood in the corridor. No. A *Wolf*. She understood it now, the difference. The size of its teeth, the huge eyes and mouth, the muscles rippling along its flank, the size of its teeth, the short stocky but powerful legs, the size of its fucking *teeth*.

Penfold closed the door, realising it was utterly futile, but not knowing what else to do.

"Is that my dad?" Josh whispered beside her. Bailey was pale beside him.

She nodded, but said, "Not anymore, kid."

CHAPTER 15

1

Knowles forced himself to stop thinking about the spiders, but it wasn't easy. He knew they wouldn't hurt him as long as he didn't try for the bones, hell, they probably wouldn't even come anywhere near him, but still—

Everything about them was *wrong*.

Had these guys got to the bones? *Used* them, like Bryant had done on purpose and Jack by accident.

So, were there three Originals on the ground now?

He risked a look over his shoulder, but the tunnel behind was empty.

Come on Penfold. Hurry up.

A muffled shout made him turn fully back to face tunnel to the house. *What was that?* Another shout, then a noise that made his blood run cold.

A howl.

2

The Wolf stopped by the pantry door, sniffing the air. It turned its baleful gaze towards the kitchen, seeing Penfold cowering at the door, aiming a weapon at him. *The boy is there. He smells like us but is not us.*

Leave him alone.

The other voice was so small it was pitiful. If it could have laughed, the Wolf would have.

Everyone is fair game here, Jack.

Everyone.

NO!

It turned away and entered the pantry.

3

Knowles knew something was wrong. He watched the tunnel but couldn't see anything moving. No sign of Penfold or Bailey, just the lights and the pools of darkness between them. The men on the ground still hadn't moved, but the howl from behind filled him with dread. Jack never howled except –

Except when he couldn't control the Wolf.

"Fuck."

Behind him, unseen, Potter sat up.

4

Potter was alert in seconds, all his focus on Knowles, who still hadn't noticed him. His CO. The man who had sent him to this life. What had he really expected to happen when Potter was faced with such power?

Knowles was a prick. So arrogant. The way he always survived. The way he let everyone else die so he could take the glory. The way he ordered people around.

He deserved to die.

Potter would be doing the world a service. He stood, feeling stronger than ever. As he stepped forward, Knowles turned, hitting him in the stomach with a full-on roundhouse kick.

The kick caught him off guard. That was the only reason he stumbled. It should have sent him crashing across the cavern, but it didn't. Of course not. He was far too strong now. Potter grinned, but then his feet slipped in the blood on the ground. He tumbled back towards the rear of the cavern.

Potter groaned as he hit the wall, air rushing out of his lungs but he was already recovering, power coursing through him. Then he saw Knowles raise his weapon and aim down the sights.

In front of him, Harry sat up.

5

Knowles was surprised the kick worked, and he watched as Potter hit the rear wall. He grunted as the air rushed out of his lungs, but Knowles knew he would recover quickly. Groans from the other two men dragged his focus towards them.

Originals.

He knew he shouldn't have come back to Devon, back to Huntleigh.

I'm fucked.

6

Harry felt different, as in a not-entirely-sure-how-just-*different* kind of way. He groaned, pushing himself to a sitting position. His hand didn't hurt which was his first surprise. The second was the man standing in front of him.

You need to get up.

He stood, without really questioning the voice in his head as his focus was entirely on the man.

Knowles. The bogeyman. The soldier at the centre of so much hate. The man who killed Flo.

7

Knowles aimed at the man, Harry, but he changed so quickly and leapt with such a speed and ferocity that Knowles didn't have time to get even a single shot off. They hit the wall, spinning and tumbling into the tunnel. The wolf was almost too large for the confined space and struggled to get its bulk back to its feet. Dust and small loose stones trickled onto its fur. Knowles scrambled away and kicked at the wolf, feet hitting its head and chest repeatedly.

Frantically he looked for his weapon and spotted it with dismay. It was *there*, underneath the wolf. *I'm still fucked.* He felt something move behind him: a movement of air perhaps, or a sixth sense developed from years in war zones. Potter was moving, recovered from his slip in blood and now leapt at him.

Knowles did the only thing he could.

He jumped towards Harry, away from Potter, rolling on the hard rock and snatching his weapon up. Teeth missed him by millimetres, huge jaws snapping at air rather than flesh. Knowles squeezed the trigger as he came out of the roll. He swept the weapon back and forth. Bullets sprayed aimlessly, the roar of the weapon deafening in the confined space.

He had to hit something, given how small the area they were in, so he kept his finger on the trigger.

He had to hit something.

Right?

8

Harry yelped as bullets tore into him, but he somehow missed the worst of it. More stones and dust fell from the ceiling and he had a moment of panic that the roof was collapse. He couldn't think of that though – there were far more pressing concerns. Potter yelped and howled as bullets tore into his flank, blowing holes in his wolf flesh. Blood poured from the wounds and Harry could see muscle, bone and sinew glistening in the holes in his body. Potter's cries galvanised Harry and he turned towards Knowles, who had his back to Harry.

He killed Flo.

Time for him to pay.

9

The Wolf sprinted, relieved to be released of its shackles. It didn't need its keen hearing to know shots were fired, or the resulting cries from its brethren.

Not brethren.

Competition.

It saw the soldier kneeling on the floor, firing indiscriminately around the cavern. Flashes from the muzzle gave the scene a strobe effect, and the Wolf watched an unknown wolf dance as bullets smashed it apart.

Knowles. He's your friend, yes?

Silence from the other and the Wolf relaxed. It had finally managed to bury *him*.

Knowles hadn't seen the other wolf stand behind him. His focus was entirely on the one in front of him. The Wolf increased its pace, the rock blurring beneath its massive paws.

This was going to be close.

10

"Holy shit!" Bailey said. "What the fuck do we do now?"

Penfold ran to the pantry door, aiming down the sights of her weapon. Jack had already disappeared into the tunnel. She heard the echoes and bangs of a weapon being discharged.

"Knowles is in trouble," she said. "Stay here."

With that, she ran after Jack, boots thumping on the wooden steps.

"What about my dad?"

Bailey looked down at Josh, taking in his pale, serious expression. *He can't lose another parent today.*

"Listen, Squiggs, you need to stay here. Your dad can take care of himself, but my friend is in trouble."

"Stay here?" Josh frowned, glancing over at the corpses on the kitchen floor. "With them?"

"They're not going anywhere."

"Where are you going?"

Bailey knelt in front of him and put a hand on his shoulder. "I'm going to help my friends. Please stay here, Josh. Please."

Without waiting to see if he complied, Bailey ran after Penfold.

11

"Stay the fuck down!" Knowles roared, as rounds poured into Potter's torso and head. Potter's skull exploded, showering the rear wall with brains and other viscera. Without pausing, Knowles turned, looking for Harry. The other wolf was just at the edge of the cavern, hunkered down, keeping itself low to avoid the onslaught of rounds.

Knowles aimed, wondering why the wolf didn't attack, but then it came to him.

There was a third person in the cavern.

Behind him.

Knowles felt breath on the back of his neck, felt drool drip onto his shoulder, felt his knees give way.

With almost comical slowness, he turned to face the wolf towering over him.

12

The Wolf leapt.

13

Knowles wasn't really sure how he survived, but here he was, still breathing. *For now. Keep going. Survive the next minute. See what happens.* The Wolf hit the brown wolf hard, sending them both crashing to the ground near Harry. Knowles couldn't keep track of the mess of limbs and teeth in front of him as the wolves fought.

It was fast, ugly, and hard.

Both animals yelped and howled, but they were so wrapped around each other Knowles couldn't shoot without hitting Jack. Instead, he turned to face the other wolf, who was also mesmerised by the fight.

Knowles squeezed the trigger, but nothing happened.

He was out of ammo.

14

Harry grinned to himself. Knowles, the big bad man, was out of ammo. No rush now. He was going to enjoy this.

15

"Come on then!" Knowles roared as Harry prowled nearer to him. The wolf didn't come any closer, but its head whipped around, drawn by something in the tunnel. Knowles swung the weapon, smacking the wolf with the butt of it. He was rewarded with a satisfying crunch as something broke in the wolf, but he knew it wouldn't be long before it recovered.

He pressed forward, hitting the wolf again and again.

16

Bailey only caught up with Penfold because she stopped, and he nearly ran into her back.

"Look!"

He didn't need her to point – the tunnel was too narrow for there to be anything else to look at.

Two huge beasts were wrestling on one side of the cavern, and on the other Knowles was attempting to bash another wolf's brains in with the butt of his weapon. The two Wolves kept flashing between human and Wolf, sometimes just limbs, sometimes their whole bodies. Whenever human flesh appeared, it was always coated with blood and many of the wounds gaped open, threatening to disgorge muscles.

"Put them down!" he said, quietly so as not to alert the fighting Wolves to their presence. As if that would make any difference to the Wolf hearing – they probably smelt the human's arrival.

"One of them is your friend."

"Not anymore!"

Penfold regarded him cooly for a moment in the dim light. Her lips were a thin line, and her jaw clenched. Then she nodded and they both opened fire at the two wolves, watching the bullets smack into them.

"Knowles!" Bailey yelled. "Get out of there!"

Knowles ignored him but continued to hit the wolf. Bailey wasn't surprised: all the gunfire had probably left him deaf and he was fighting for his life.

They edged closer, weapons trained on the two wolves who now lay writhing on the ground. As Bailey approached, he saw the fur running back into the bodies, revealing Jack and another man. Both were bleeding from wounds caused by a combination of bites, claws and bullets. He could only imagine the agony they must be in.

Jack had a strip of three claw marks across his midriff, each gaping and flapping as he moved. If they were any deeper, he would be holding his guts in. His left leg was a ruined mess of torn skin, and he had chunks missing from his muscles. He screamed in agony, and Bailey could see the edges of each wound trying to knit together but he was not healing.

"Jesus," he whispered. *No way is Jack coming back from this. No way.*

He reached out, and grabbed Knowles' shirt, pulling him back from the other wolf. Knowles whirled around, eyes wide, face covered in blood. He nearly hit Bailey, but stopped himself as Bailey caught the swinging arm.

"Easy, mate."

Knowles breathed heavily, but then seemed to come back to himself. "Kill them. Kill them all."

Bailey nodded.

Behind Knowles, the wolf had turned back into a human. His face was already healing. Beyond him, Potter's head was slowly reforming as bits of his skull wriggled across the ground, slipping into place like a film in reverse.

"We need to go," Bailey said. "Now!"

17

Harry grunted and groaned as energy coursed through him.

GET UP!

Who the hell is that?

He had a voice inside him, a voice that was very definitely not his own.

Deal with it. Get the fuck up.

He pushed himself to his feet, hearing the bones of his face crunch back into place. At some point, he must have done something right because now there were two humans in front of him. A third was further back in the tunnel, watching them with her mouth open. Harry grinned to himself, despite the pain of his regeneration.

Healing was hungry work.

18

Bailey pulled Knowles back from Harry, as the man swiped at him. His fist turned into a huge paw, topped with razor sharp claws, but it whistled past, slicing the air where Knowles had just stood.

"Run!" Bailey said.

Knowles didn't need to be told twice.

19

Jack sat up. Every fibre of him felt like it was on fire. *Original bites, Jacky boy, hurts like a bitch, doesn't it?* He ignored the voice. There were more pressing concerns.

Next to him, Rich was getting to his feet.

20

Penfold was about to fire when she heard something surprising. Knowles and Bailey were coming down one side of the tunnel, hogging the right-hand side, giving her a clear shot of the wolves in the cavern.

"Dad?"

21

Josh watched the wolves lying on the floor, saw them turn into humans, then saw the horrific wounds covering his father's body as he sat up. He cried out and pushed past the nice lady soldier before she realised he was there.

He ran into the cavern, ignoring the shouts from Bailey and the woman and instead knelt by his injured father. Jack blinked fast, confusion and pain clear on his face.

"Dad!"

"Josh." Jack's breathing was laboured, every breath an effort. Blood poured from his various wounds, and he was pale, even in the dim light. Rich was standing, hand on the cavern wall, also covered with lots of cuts and open wounds.

"You need to leave, kiddo. I can't control this."

He tried to push Josh away, but his strength had gone, and he managed to press a hand to the boy's chest instead.

"No," Josh said, tears streaming down his face. "I'm not leaving you."

Rich punched Jack, hard enough to send a tooth flying and for Jack's head to whip to one side. Rich roared, black fur appearing all over his body.

"RUN!" Jack roared and he pushed Josh back with his head as it turned into the Wolf. He butted Josh again, teeth gnashing at the boy. Josh scrambled away, as teeth grazed against his arm, cutting the sleeve of his t-shirt. Strong arms grabbed him from behind and dragged him away before the Wolf could get a hold.

Josh wriggled, but Knowles was too strong and he held him fast as he pulled. "Leave him, he's not in control!" Knowles yelled. "We need to get out of here."

The third wolf, Harry, forgotten in the carnage and the fight launched himself at the pair of them.

Knowles sensed the movement before he saw it. A rush of air maybe, a sound as Harry leapt, a sixth sense developed over years of combat situations. He would never know. Knowles turned, shielding Josh with his body as Harry hit them. Knowles managed to push Josh just before Harry crashed into him and Josh stumbled and fell further into the tunnel, out of reach of Harry.

Knowles smiled as he saw Josh safely out of the wolf's range.

Yeah, time for the papers to go in.

Pain consumed him as the wolf took a chunk out of his back. He tried to crawl away, but it had him pinned. There was nothing he could do. *Backup should be here.* He watched blood spread, covering the ground around his head like a flood. His blood. *Any second.* The team would run in, shooting the wolves, drag him to safety, patch him up. Hell, maybe Penfold and Bailey would actually do something rather than just stand there with their mouths open.

More hot pain lanced through him, although conversely his legs felt cold and numb. *How the hell am I going to get out of this?* It took a moment, too long a moment, to realise he wasn't.

Fucking wolves.

Fucking Devon.

22

Potter was awake. He knew he shouldn't be, knew he should be dead, but facts were facts. He saw the fight in the cavern: Rich and Stadler fighting whilst constantly changing between human and wolf form, and he saw that Stadler was losing.

Good. The other one will be nicely softened up.

The other voice scared him at first, but he was getting used to it already. This was what he had always wanted, right? Free from disease, free from worry about an aging body, free from rules and regulations. Potter smiled to himself, despite the pain from the wounds still healing.

Out of the corner of his eye, he saw Harry take a chunk of Knowles' head off, and the smile became a giggle.

Kill them.

Kill them all.

23

"Jesus," Bailey whispered. He couldn't believe it. Knowles was on the ground and the wolf was eating his head. It had removed most of his skull and was in at his brain, eating large mouthfuls of it. Bailey knew humans could put their own emotions on animals, but it really looked like the Wolf was enjoying itself.

Penfold fired at it, and bullets hit into chest, and one took its ear off. The wolf looked up at them, mouth and teeth covered in red gore, and it continued chewing. It seemed to be grinning at them.

"Fuck this," Bailey said, and he fired a couple of rounds at the wolf too. One hit its eye, smashing through the back of its skull. The wolf collapsed on top of Knowles.

They edged forwards, keeping their weapons trained on the wolf. Bailey helped Josh to his feet.

"You okay, Squiggs?"

The boy looked groggy, his pupils much larger than they should be, even in the dim light. He'd taken a hell of a bang to the head. Blood coated one of his arms, and he wiped it, showing no cuts to the skin.

He's covered in his father's blood. Jesus Christ, how much therapy is this kid going to need? "Let's get the hell out of here."

They all backed away from the cavern, waiting for the wolf on Knowles to start moving again, but it didn't. Jack and Rich continued their fight deeper in the cavern.

"My dad." Josh said, but he continued moving with them.

"We can't help him," Bailey said. He knew the truth of that. Sure, they could shoot, but the way the two men fight meant there was no way they could get a clear shot. If they fired, they would have to take them both out. Besides, with those wounds, both men would bleed out before too much longer. They were slowing down, each punch or bite a fraction slower than before.

"How many rounds you got?" Penfold asked. "I'm nearly out."

"Me too."

"Then let's get out of here. Backup should be here any minute."

They turned and ran down the tunnel, heading for the sanctuary of the house.

Behind them, unseen and ignored, Potter gave chase.

24

Rich was on top of him, both physically and metaphorically. Jack knew he was losing this fight, and no-one was coming to save him. He saw Bailey and Josh run away, and he didn't blame them. *Please get my son safe. Please.*

Rich was in human form, punching him repeatedly. Black dots swam at the edge of Jack's vision, becoming bigger with every blow.

Get up, Jack.

Kill him. Kill him for what he did to Katie.

Jack let the Wolf take over, and he turned, the Wolf bursting free of its shackles once more. Despite the wounds, it still had reserves of strength and it opened its mouth. Rich punched, not seeing the change come over Jack's mouth and his fist slid into its gaping maw rather than hitting its cheek.

The Wolf bit down, severing Rich's hand at the wrist. Rich howled and fell back, freeing the Wolf. Limbs protesting at the exertion, the

Wolf pressed its advantage and jumped on Rich, managing to get hold of his neck for the first time. It whipped its head up, bringing a chunk of neck with it.

Rich choked and gargled, hands flying to his neck, but it was too late. Blood poured from the wound, and he was helpless to stop it.

Jack returned, forcing the Wolf away. "For my wife," he said.

25

You lost.

Rich had already come to hate the voice.

You lost to a fucking teacher.

Rich pawed at his neck, trying to hold the blood in with his remaining hand, trying to hold on to life, even though he knew it was futile. Movement behind Jack caught his eye, and at first, he thought it was a result of blood loss, but no, dark shapes were moving there.

Despite everything, Rich grinned. He wasn't making it out of here, but then, neither was Jack fucking Stadler.

26

Searing pain roared up Bailey's legs and back as something hit him from behind. He spun in the air, landing heavily on his back with all the air forced out of his lungs. Something snapped and this time it wasn't pain, but agony that coursed through him. He was about to ask what had happened when he got his answer.

A wolf grabbed Penfold and wrestled her to the ground. She screamed and slapped at it, but it was no use. The wolf ripped her tunic open and bit into her stomach, pulling out a coil of intestines.

Bailey looked at his leg and saw bone sticking through his jeans. *Shit. Not running anywhere now.* Ahead of him, Josh stopped, turning to face him. Bailey shook his head, motioning for Josh to run on. The boy ignored him, continuing to come back to Bailey.

The wolf raised its head, teeth bared at the approaching boy. A low growl came from it.

"Run, Josh!" Bailey yelled, speaking harshly to the boy for the first time ever. Then, to the wolf, "Over here, dickhead."

The wolf's head snapped around, glaring at Bailey with its baleful eyes.

"Come get me, motherfucker."

The wolf pounced, and Bailey pulled the pin from the grenade in his pocket.

27

Jack sank back to the floor, all of him back to human form. Exhaustion married the pain coursing through him, making it nearly impossible to move. The Wolf wanted out again, to finish the job on Rich, but there wasn't any need.

Rich was dying. Originals could hurt other Originals. Jack had known that since his fight with Bryant, but he hadn't realised the bites could be fatal. Rich writhed on the floor in front of Jack, holding his neck, desperately trying to stop the flow of blood from the wound, but he was leaking blood from his severed wrist too. Those wounds were not healing anytime soon, even with Original blood. The skin around the gaping hole in his neck flapped like pieces of a ripped flag in the wind, but they were not knitting together. Maybe they would in time, but it wouldn't be quick enough for Rich.

Jack thought he would feel more, watching the man who killed Katie die, but he felt empty. Too much pain. Too tired.

Rich gurgled again, and lunged at Jack, landing on his chest. He lay on Jack, letting his blood fall over Jack's face, as he tried to laugh. Jack tried to push him away but couldn't. His arms felt like lead.

A scraping noise to his right, followed by another and another. Jack closed his eyes.

The spiders had arrived, and they crawled over both men. Jack thought he was in pain, until the first one bit him and then a whole new world of agony exploded inside him.

NO!

The Wolf howled in frustration and terror inside him. He'd never heard it sound like that before, not even in the early days before he could control it. It continued screaming inside him, but neither had the energy to fight what was happening as the spiders swarmed over both him and Rich. Is this what had happened to the first Original? The one laying on that strange altar in the cave he'd fallen into all those years before. Had it been weakened enough for the spiders to attack? Jack was in too much pain to really care. He saw a group of spiders poured down the tunnel, covering Harry in seconds.

Jack's final thoughts were of Josh. He would never see his son grow up. Never see him go on his first date. Take him driving. Hold a grandson or daughter. However, Josh had escaped, and for that, Jack was grateful.

At least his son wouldn't see both parents die today.

28

Josh ran. He didn't understand what was happening, but he knew he had to get away. Adrenaline gave him the extra reserve he needed to sprint away from Bailey, even though his legs screamed and protested. He was nearly at the stairs when the grenade exploded.

EPILOGUE

The boy sat whilst soldiers ran around him, looking like ants from an exposed nest. He looked at his arm, marvelling at the smooth, unbroken skin. His clothes had ripped in several places, and dust from the collapsing tunnel covered him.

A man came over, blonde hair, blue eyes, green uniform. He smelled of cheap aftershave and tobacco. He carried a big bag with *Medic* written on the side and he crouched next to the boy.

"Hey kid, I'm Roy. What's your name?"

The boy told him, and he thought his voice had never sounded so far away, so lacking in life.

"Okay, kid. Let's have a look at you." Roy did the light thing in his eyes, checked his limbs, and moved a finger left to right in front of him. Satisfied, he nodded. "You look in good shape, kiddo. Do you know where your parents are?"

"Dead."

Roy paled a little at that and looked uncomfortable. He shifted his weight but didn't stand.

"Okay, uh, um, we'll get someone on that. Is there someone we can call?"

The boy shook his head and Roy looked like he'd rather be anywhere than right here.

"At least you're not hurt." It sounded lame, even to him.

"No, I'm not," the boy said. Roy stood, nodded twice, looking ridiculous and awkward, and then he left, pretending he'd seen someone else needing his attention.

Well done.

The voice came from somewhere inside him, loud and full of humour.

Don't tell anyone. This can be our little secret.

The boy nodded agreement, even though no-one could hear the conversation but him.

I'll look after you, don't worry.

The boy felt tears well at the thought of his dad.

I'll take very good care of us.

He stood and walked away from the soldiers, heading out to the road.

THE END

ACKNOWLEDGEMENTS

Most people skip this bit in a book, but I always read them. It fascinates me how books are written by one person, but there is always a team around that person, helping them in a number of ways. This book is no exception, so read on and find the team that helped make this a reality. Hell, maybe you'll see your name.

First off, thanks to my wonderful family. You give me the space and time to do this, which is no small thing given I also work full-time. So, Tinu, Josh and Ethan, you are my rocks and I love you beyond words. Yes, Katie and Josh are based on you, and yes, I'm sorry for what I put you through in this book.

Rich Evans and Dave Jeffery were kind enough to read early versions of this and the book is stronger for your help and comments. Rich has been a long-time supporter of what I do, so I'm sorry about the 'pantry' jibe in the book. Dave Jeffery is a wonderful writer (the pilot is reading one of his books, *A Quiet Apocalypse*. Go check it out. Thank me later.) and extremely supportive of indie authors in the genre. He's also a top bloke, which I rate more highly than anything else. Cheers Dave, and yes, it's my round.

Thanks are also due to Rowan Kendall-Torry for the photograph on the front cover. Nailed it as usual my friend. Frank from gfivedesign worked his magic to make Rowan's photo look suitably sinister and was very patient with my picky changes. Cathy Farenden designed the logos for Original Books and she is a lovely, talented lady I am proud to call a friend. Dan Howarth did a sterling job on the interior design, and he is also a wonderful writer in his own right.

Another writer mentioned early in this book is Kit Power. He's another person who is a great guy and wonderful writer. Years ago, he invited me to do a reading at an event, which was a huge confidence boost for me as I was fairly certain no-one knew who I was at the time. The other writers on the bill that night were Charlotte Bond, Phil Sloman, Laura Mauro and CC Adams as well as Kit himself. Ha, now you have more writers to check out and you should. That'll teach you for reading the acknowledgements.

The other two Original's books were written with the technical help of my old friend Ed. For reasons unknown, he always wanted to be credited as Pat. Sadly, Ed committed suicide recently, and whilst I hadn't seen him in a while, his loss still hit me hard. Rest easy big guy.

Finally, to everyone who has ever read, reviewed or talked about one of my books, a huge thank you. I never for a moment thought my books would be read by so many people, and the fact they seem to be well liked is massively humbling (and more than a little terrifying when you're trying to write the third book in a never-meant-to-be trilogy).

In the ever-so-slightly sinister words of an old student of mine (Alfie Weldon, you legend): until next time.

Dave Watkins

February 2024

ALSO BY DAVID WATKINS

The Original's Series:
The Original's Return
The Original's Retribution
The Original, short story in Leaders of The Pack (pub. Horrific Tales)

Stand alone:
The Devil's Inn
The Exeter Incident (pub D & T publishing)

If you have enjoyed these, or any other books by indie authors, please
leave a review and talk about it on social media – it really does make
all the difference.
Thank you for reading this far!

www.ingramcontent.com/pod-product-compliance
Lightning Source LLC
Chambersburg PA
CBHW071458170626
46811CB00007B/2628